Books by Natalie Babbitt

The Search for Delicious

The SEARCH
for
DELICIOUS

Natalie Babbitt

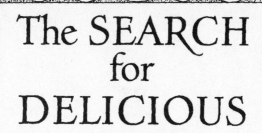

SQUARE
FISH

Farrar, Straus and Giroux

SQUARE
FISH

An Imprint of Macmillan

Square Fish and the Square Fish logo are trademarks of Macmillan and are used by Farrar Straus Giroux under license from Macmillan.

Library of Congress Catalog Card Number: 69-20374

ISBN 978-0-312-36982-8

Originally published in the United States by Farrar Straus Giroux
Square Fish logo designed by Filomena Tuosto
First Square Fish Edition: August 2007
10 9 8
mackids.com

AR: 5.4 / F&P:U / LEXILE: 910L

How Gaylen Searched
the Kingdom for Delicious

PROLOGUE

HERE WAS A TIME ONCE when the earth was still very young, a time some call the oldest days. This was long before there were any people about to dig parts of it up and cut parts of it off. People came along much later, building their towns and castles (which nearly always fell down after a while) and plaguing each other with quarrels and supper parties. The creatures who lived on the earth in that early time stayed each in his own place and kept it beautiful. There were dwarfs in the mountains, woldwellers in the forests, mermaids in the lakes, and, of course, winds in the air.

There was one particular spot on the earth where a ring of mountains enclosed a very dry and dusty place. There were winds and dwarfs there, but no mermaids because there weren't any lakes, and there were no woldwellers either because forests couldn't grow in so dry a place.

Then a remarkable thing happened. Up in the mountains one day a dwarf was poking about with a sharp tool, looking for a good spot to begin mining. He poked and poked until he had made a very deep hole in the earth. Then he poked again and clear spring water came spurting up in the hole. He hurried in great excitement to tell the other dwarfs and they all came running to see the water. They were so pleased with it that they built over it a fine house of heavy stones and they made a special door out of a flat rock and balanced it in its place very carefully on carved hinges. Then one of them made a whistle out of a small stone which blew a certain very high note tuned to just the right warble so that when you blew it, the door of the rock house would open, and when you blew it again, the door would shut. They took turns being in charge of the whistle and they worked hard to keep the spring clean and beautiful.

But the spring they had discovered was in a cup of land surrounded by cliffs and eventually the spring began to fill up the cup, until after a while there was a little lake there with the top of the spring house standing out in the center like an island. And the lake kept getting higher and higher. After a few years the spring house was completely submerged and the dwarfs could no longer get down to it, although they could see it easily through the clear water and could still make the door open and close with the whistle, just the same as before.

The water in the lake began in time to fill up with creatures of its own, as water has a way of doing, and one of these creatures was a lovely little mermaid. The dwarfs named her Ardis and one of them made her a pretty doll out of linked stones with a trailing fern fastened to its head for hair. Ardis loved the doll very much and played with it all the time, and in exchange she promised to keep watch over the spring in the house of rocks, now far down under the water. So the dwarfs gave her the special whistle and she kept it hanging by a chain on a sharp bit of rock at the water's edge. Every morning she would blow the whistle to open the door and then she would dive down and play with her doll

ng the bubbles. At night she would come up
he whistle again to close the door, and swim
away to sleep.

While all this was happening, the water in the lake
had risen so high that it began to spill over in one spot
where there was a V-shaped gap in the cliffs, and it
tumbled down into the dry and dusty place ringed by
the mountains. It fingered itself into a great many
streams and watered the land so well that everything
was soon green and fresh. Forests sprang up and woldwellers came there to watch over the trees. And then,
later, the people began to arrive. They built towns and
they crowned a king and they enjoyed a great many
quarrels and troubles, all of which they created quite
by themselves. The dwarfs withdrew deep under the
mountains where they wouldn't have to watch and they
went on mining and almost never came out. In time
they separated into groups of two or three, each group
mining where it chose, and they never lived all together
again. The woldwellers, who were admired by the people for their knowledge, stayed in their trees and came
down to answer questions from time to time, but after

a while they grew irritated by the foolishness of these questions and wouldn't always answer. Eventually the people stopped coming to ask.

And something very sad happened to Ardis. One day, when she was in the spring house playing with her doll, she heard a new and pleasing kind of sound. She put down the doll and swam up to the top of the lake. There on the bank sat a man, the first she had ever seen, making pretty music on a round box with strings pulled tight across it. Ardis stayed to listen, hiding behind a water lily, with only her eyes and ears out of the water. After a while the man put the round box aside and, leaning over to drink from the lake, noticed the whistle hanging from its sharp bit of rock. He picked it up and blew through it, but he was only a man and couldn't hear the sound it made. As Ardis watched in dismay, he started to toss it away, paused, looked at it again, and finally hung it around his neck. Then he picked up his strange instrument and wandered off. She cried to him to come back, but he didn't hear.

Ardis dove trembling to the spring house, but the blast the man had blown on the whistle had made the door swing shut. The house was locked. Ardis could peer through the cracks between the rocks and see her doll lying inside, but there was no way to get it out. After that, she was sad all the time. At night she would swim up to the spot where the whistle had hung, and weep for hours. Someone heard her once and made a song about her, but no one could help her, for the dwarfs were far away.

And in the meantime, in the land below, towns were built and burned and built again and kings and their people lived and died and enjoyed their troubles for years and years and years. Ardis and the dwarfs and the woldwellers were largely forgotten except in stories and songs. Nobody believed they were real any more except for an occasional child or an even more occasional worker of evil, these being the only ones with imagination enough to admit to the possibility of something even more amazing in the world than those commonplace marvels which it spreads so carelessly before us every day.

IN HIS WORKROOM AT THE top of the tower, DeCree, the Prime Minister, was pacing up and down. Occasionally he would pause, throw up his arms in a gesture of helplessness, and then resume his pacing. From her perch, his cockatoo watched with beady interest, turning her head this way and that as he crossed and recrossed before her.

"There will be civil war!" he burst out at last. "Splits, upheavals, and people taking sides! Smiles will be forgotten and spring will escape notice! Little flowers will push up, only to be trodden down, and birds will sing unheeded."

From a pile of cushions in a corner of the room, his Special Assistant, a skinny, pleasant boy of twelve named Gaylen, put down the book he had been reading and frowned. "Civil war?" he said. "But why? What happened?"

"It was like this," said the Prime Minister, climbing onto the stool at his desk. "I went down, you see, to show the King how far I've gone on my dictionary. He was pleased with the first part. He liked 'Affectionate is your dog' and 'Annoying is a loose boot in a muddy place' and so on, and he smiled at 'Bulky is a big bag of boxes.' As a matter of fact, there was no trouble with any of the A's or B's and the C's were fine too, especially 'Calamitous is saying no to the King.' But then we got to 'Delicious is fried fish' and he said no, I'd have to change that. He doesn't care for fried fish. The General of the Armies was standing there and he said that, as far as he was concerned, Delicious is a mug of beer, and the Queen said no, Delicious is a Christmas pudding, and then the King said nonsense, everyone knew the most delicious thing is an apple, and they all began quarreling. Not just the three of them—the whole court. When I left, they were all yelling and shouting and shaking their fists. The King and the General were glaring at each other, and the Queen was trying to get everyone to listen to the recipe for Christmas pudding."

"That doesn't sound like civil war to me," said Gaylen, turning back to his book with a smile. "It only sounds silly."

"Of course it's silly," said the Prime Minister impatiently. "But a lot of serious things start silly."

Gaylen put his book down again and sighed. "Why don't you just leave Delicious out of the dictionary?"

"I can't do that," said the Prime Minister. "If this is going to be a proper dictionary, I can't leave anything out."

At that moment there was a great racket in the courtyard below. Gaylen ran to the window and looked down. People were pouring out of the castle door to form a noisy ring around two men shoving each other about on the grass. After a moment, one knocked the other flat, shouted "Plums!" and strode triumphantly back inside, followed by the cheering crowd. The man who had been flattened swayed to his feet and went off muttering.

The Prime Minister shook his head sadly. "Now here's a pretty kettle of fish," he said.

"Or apples," said Gaylen.

GAYLEN HAD LIVED IN THE castle ever since he'd been left, a tiny baby, gurgling in a basket at the main gate. The basket had been carried in to the King, who was very annoyed to see its contents.

"Now, by Harry," the King had said with a frown, "I suppose some silly mother thinks I'll adopt this baby and leave the kingdom to him when I die. Well, I won't do it. I expect to have a son of my own some day. Take this baby away and see if one of the kitchen maids will have it."

But the Prime Minister was hovering nearby and sprang forward when he heard what the King was saying. "Please, your Majesty, let *me* have the baby," he said. "I'll take good care of him, and I promise he'll never be a bother to you."

"Humph!" said the King. "What on earth do *you* want a baby for? Well, go ahead. Take it. Why not?" So the Prime Minister went joyfully off with the basket and the King promptly forgot all about it.

Now the truth is that DeCree was a very lonely man. He had never had a wife, and he lived all by himself in the castle tower. But it wasn't a wife he was lonely for, it was a child. He wanted a child so badly that it kept him awake thinking about it. And when he couldn't sleep, he got overtired and caught colds and went about snuffling, with his beard wrapped around his throat to keep it warm. It made him feel achy and wretched and when he went to advise the King on important matters, he would say things like "Dow thed" for "Now then," and "Dot eddy bore" for "Not any more." When he did this, the King would get cross, and that made the Prime Minister feel worse than ever.

But after the baby came to live with him in the tower, the Prime Minister slept nine hours every night without even snoring and he was never lonely again. So he named the baby Vaungaylen, which means "little healer." It was a very long name, so the baby was mostly called Gaylen for short, which suited him very well, and as soon as he was old enough, the Prime Minister taught him to read and write and made him Special Assistant. And if Gaylen came to believe that the world was a bright and flawless garden where no weeds grew, a garden in the center of which the castle tower rose high and watchful and serene, it was not to be wondered at. After all, he was cared for very tenderly, with never a wish ungratified, and he and the

Prime Minister loved each other as much as any real father and son since time began.

THAT NIGHT THE CONVERSA-tion around the King's dinner table was strained. Nobody was letting anybody forget the arguments of the afternoon.

"What's for dinner tonight?" said the King to the Queen with a broad smile. "Apples, I hope?"

"Dear me, no," said the Queen in a bored tone. "Not apples again. One gets so very tired of them."

"Well, at least, seeing as it's nearly spring," said the King through his teeth, "I don't suppose we'll have to sit through a Christmas pudding."

The Queen turned away with a toss of her head and spoke to the General, who sat nearby. "Wine, General?"

"Beer or nothing!" he answered grimly.

Just then the royal dinner was carried in, a huge roast of venison with carrots and potatoes and a variety of fruits in bowls. The guests began muttering to each other about the meal. Everyone was dissatisfied with it in one way or another, but the Prime Minister rose and bowed to the Queen. "An excellent dinner, your Majesty," he said politely. "I'm sure we'll all enjoy it enormously."

"Even without fried fish?" asked the Queen, glaring at him.

"Well, of course," answered the Prime Minister in an effort to be generous, "one can't eat fried fish every night."

"One can't eat fried fish any night *at all* unless one

is a troublemaking old fool," said the King flatly.

The Prime Minister sat down abruptly and closed his eyes.

"Very well, then," came a deep voice from the end of the table, "where are the nuts? The walnuts, the chestnuts, the pecans?" It was the voice of Hemlock, a brother to the Queen, who stood at his place scowling. "Where, I say, are the nuts? We always have nuts for dinner."

"We never have nuts for dinner," said the King, "starting now."

Hemlock smiled dangerously. He was a tall, unpleasant man and a friend to no one, not even his sister the Queen. He reached into his pockets and pulled out two large handfuls of nuts, which he threw high into the air. Then he turned and left the room. The nuts came raining down on the tabletop, splashed into the wine and bounced off the heads of the guests, who rose in a body, with a great deal of noise and confusion.

When the King had restored order at last and everyone was sitting down again, he thumped on the table with his fist. "See here," he said, "this cannot continue! Now, where has Hemlock gone?" He looked around, frowning. "Well, let him go. Things always seem more peaceful without him. And anyway, DeCree started all this and he'll have to find a way to settle it." He looked at the Prime Minister. "Well?" he said.

"Well," said the Prime Minister hopefully, "we could just forget all about it."

"No," said the King, "we couldn't."

"Then," said the Prime Minister, "we'll have to find out what everybody thinks and write it all down and then whatever gets the most votes for Delicious will be the thing I use in the dictionary."

"That's a very good idea, DeCree," said the King. "Go all around the kingdom and ask everybody. It'll turn out to be apples, anyway."

"Beer," said the General.

"Pudding," murmured the Queen.

The King looked as if he were going to lose his temper, but he gritted his teeth and managed to pull himself together. "Start right away on this journey, DeCree," he said. "There's no time to lose."

"But I can't go myself," protested the Prime Minister. "I'm too old for a long trip like that."

"Then who shall go?" asked the King in some alarm. "Whom can we trust?"

"I'll send my assistant, Vaungaylen," said the Prime Minister.

"Well, all right," said the King, "as long as he's trustworthy."

"He's an upright and honest boy," said the Prime Minister firmly, "and the apple of my eye."

"The *pudding*," murmured the Queen.

"Now, by Harry," the King began angrily, and then paused. Someone was galloping across the courtyard below and on over the drawbridge. The King went to a window and peered out. "There goes Hemlock," he announced. "He's riding that big gray horse of his, Ballywrack. Well, maybe he'll stay away. I wish he would, by Harry. He's always trying to take over and run things." He went back to his place at the table and looked severely at the assembled guests. "Too many cooks spoil the soup, you know," he said.

"Too many cooks spoil the *pudding*," murmured the Queen.

THE NEXT MORNING EVERYone gathered in the courtyard to see Gaylen start off. He had been well equipped and instructed by the Prime Minister and knew exactly what to do. There was a large notebook in his saddlebag, and pens and ink, the proclamation he was to read to the people, and a map of the kingdom. It was not very large, as kingdoms go, perhaps thirty miles square, and there were four towns. It was on the basis of this number that DeCree and the King had decided to allow four weeks to complete the poll.

"Four weeks if he's trustworthy, that is," said the

King to the Prime Minister, whom he had drawn to one side.

"I raised him myself," said DeCree, "and he's true to the core."

"I hope so," said the King. "There's something about this whole business that makes me nervous."

"You don't need to worry about Vaungaylen," said the Prime Minister.

"Well, maybe," said the King suspiciously. "Maybe. What's his choice for Delicious?"

"He hasn't said," replied the Prime Minister.

"Just as well," said the King. He turned back to where Gaylen sat high on a fine horse, waiting to start off. The horse, whose name was Marrow, was one of the King's best and was draped in the royal colors. "Here, boy," said the King to Gaylen. "Here's a little something to munch along the way." And he handed up a sack of apples. Gaylen said thank you and stowed the apples away in his saddlebag, alongside the packet of cold fried fish and the sheaf of recipes for Christmas pudding.

"And now," said the King to the assembled company, "before this boy starts out to poll the people, I want to make one thing quite clear. All of you here at the castle are going to stay here at the castle. There'll be no running ahead to buy up votes for this or that. We'll all stay here quietly for the four weeks and we'll talk of other things."

"That's right," said the Prime Minister. "That's the only way to handle it. Good luck, Gaylen, and I'll send my cockatoo after you with the news each Wednesday and Saturday."

"You're off then," said the King, and he gave Marrow a slap. The horse went booming over the draw-bridge and everybody cheered. They went on cheering until horse and rider had disappeared over a grassy hill and down through a stand of hornbeams, where the first road led to the first town. It all seemed very like a holiday and Gaylen, bouncing up and down on Marrow's broad back, was excited and happy. To ride out on a strong horse and to see the kingdom—this was very fine, indeed.

"You've lived too long here with me in the castle," the Prime Minister had said to him earlier that morning. "It will be good for you to go about and see something of what the world is really like while you're still young enough not to get discouraged."

Gaylen had gazed wide-eyed through the tower window at the broad land stretching away toward its ring of mountains through the young green mists of early spring. "I don't see why I should get discouraged," he had answered. "After all, I'm twelve years old. I know what the world is like and I can take care of myself."

"Yes, I suppose you can," said the Prime Minister, laying his arm gently about the boy's shoulders and peering out beside him. "Well, well, perhaps I'm only being gloomy. I suppose I'm getting old." He had brightened then and rumpled Gaylen's hair. "You'll have splendid adventures, boy. Let's go and get you ready."

And now here he was, jogging briskly along in the golden morning sun, proud and straight in the saddle, ready for anything, he told himself, and hopeful for much. He reached happily into his saddlebag and took out one of the King's apples. But when he bit into it, his teeth struck painfully on something very hard. He drew back sharply and peered at the apple. A portion of the skin had been peeled back and someone had cut out a bit of the fruit and forced in a walnut. "Hemlock," he said to himself. "Hemlock did that." He stared at the apple for a moment and a shivery feeling twinkled down his spine. Then he threw the apple as far as he could into the underbrush and spurred Marrow forward. "Silly," he said to himself, and he began to whistle a little tune. The tune was merry and the morning was sweet and soon the apple and its burden were far from his mind.

I T WAS NOON WHEN GAYLEN rode into the first town. The streets were noisy with people going about their usual business, but when they saw Gaylen and the royal draperies on the horse, they left what they were doing and followed along behind him in a buzz of curiosity. Gaylen rode straight to the square in the center of town and cried out, as he had been told to do, "Gather round! Gather round! I'm here on the King's business!" In no time at all, the entire population of the town had crowded into the square and the Mayor himself was elbowing his way through to where Gaylen sat on his horse. There was a considerable racket, what with everyone shoving and laughing, but the Mayor climbed up on the well that stood there and raised his hand.

"This uproar is downright disgraceful!" he bellowed. "Everyone be quiet or you'll all go to jail!"

In the hush that followed, Gaylen read the proclamation in a loud, clear voice:

Let it be known that every single creature in my kingdom who is capable of speech shall register with my messenger the following information: name, age, home, and the food he or she honestly believes to be the most delicious of all foods.

Gaylen rolled up the proclamation and added, "Now,

if you'll all just form into a long line, we'll get on with the listing," and he took the large notebook and his pen and ink out of the saddlebag.

The people began happily jostling one another into a sort of line. Since there were nearly two hundred present, counting the children, there was a great deal of confusion. But this was not the worst of it, for of course the people got to discussing the proclamation and it wasn't two minutes before they began arguing. Gaylen had barely registered three names when a scuffle broke out somewhere in the middle of the line—a scuffle which rapidly became a fist fight, a fist fight which immediately developed into a general free-for-all. The whole square had suddenly become one big grappling mass of people, all throwing things and punching one another and falling down and tearing one another's clothes and yelling things like "Melons!" and "Pork!" and "Raisin cake!" The Mayor, who was still standing on the well beside Gaylen and the horse, tried to salvage a shred of order, but his yells only added to the general din. At last he climbed up behind Gaylen and shouted into his ear, "Come on! I'll have to call out the Guard."

Marrow carried them off through the square, dodging flying vegetables and trying not to step on anybody. They stopped on a side street before a little building where a sign said MAYOR in large letters. "Just a minute while I call out the Guard," said the Mayor, and he drew a deep breath. Then he bellowed at the top of his lungs: "GUARD! I say, GUARD!"

In response to this ear-splitting summons, a soldier in a battered leather jerkin and helmet appeared at the door. He carried a long spear, around the point of which had been tied a small pillow.

"What's the pillow for?" asked Gaylen.

"Well, we don't want to hurt anyone, you know," said the Mayor. "Now then, go up there and calm everybody down," he said to the soldier, "and tell them all to come in here one by one. Tell them it's the King's command."

The soldier trudged off and the Mayor took Gaylen into his office. "It makes me feel a whole lot better, having a Guard to call out at a time like this," he said, sinking into his chair behind a large table. "But it's most upsetting, to say the least. What on earth does the King want to go and stir up a lot of trouble for?"

"Well, you see," said Gaylen, "the Prime Minister is writing a dictionary and he's having a hard time with a definition for Delicious. That's all it is. I can't see why everyone gets so excited about it."

"Oh, people enjoy getting excited, you know," said the Mayor. "But just the same, it's different this time. There's something in the air. I had a report this morning that there's a fellow riding about talking against the King. I hope he doesn't try to come here. By George, I do. It's possible that, on the whole, part of it could be an overall undercurrent of dissatisfaction. If the King lies down on the job, the people will stand to gain a loss of confidence in him. Mark my words, in the end it will be the beginning of trouble!" And he sighed and gazed out the window.

Gaylen thought he understood what the Mayor was trying to say. His thoughts turned to the brawling people in the square beyond, whose shouts and cries could still be heard, and he was reminded suddenly of the walnut in the King's apple. The morning's holiday mood was gone and in its place was a vague uneasiness, like the feeling you get when you run down the road to overtake a friend and find, when he turns to meet you, that it isn't a friend at all but a stranger.

IT WAS THREE DAYS BEFORE everyone in the town had been registered, and when the job was finished, Gaylen turned over the pages of the notebook and sighed. If the poll continued like this, he said to himself, the Prime Minister would have to leave out Delicious whether he would or no, for so far no two votes agreed, and some of them were very complicated. The only mention of apples, for instance, came in the form of a vote for apple tarts, but apple tarts baked with nutmeg, not cinnamon, and, even then, really delicious only when served with sharp yellow cheese. You couldn't put a definition like that into a dictionary.

He put the notebook away in his saddlebag and crossed from the office to the Mayor's house, where for the last time he would spend the night. He was glad to be finished with polling the town, but the evenings had been fine, for the Mayor had a little daughter named Medley and every night he told her stories. Gaylen had sat two evenings, his eyes as wide as Medley's, while the Mayor wove tales of wise fish and heroes, elusive white roebucks and castles of the dead, long and remarkable tales that left you breathless; but he tried not to let the Mayor see how eagerly he listened. After all, he was nearly grown. Still, stories like these were never heard in the castle unless a passing minstrel stopped to sing. He loved them, marveled at them, half believed them. And wanted to believe them altogether.

"What shall it be tonight, Medley?" asked the

Mayor that evening after supper. "Dwarfs? Or mermaids?"

"Please, Papa," she said, climbing up beside him, "tell us a story about the woldweller."

"Us?"

"Yes, Gaylen and me. He likes the stories, too."

"What's a woldweller?" asked Gaylen quickly, frowning at Medley and hoping the Mayor wouldn't make a pointed remark.

"Dear me!" said the Mayor. "A great boy like you and you don't know about woldwellers? Well, then. A woldweller, so the legend goes, is a creature who lives all alone up in a tree in the forest. A little inmate of the great outdoors, you might say. He is very, very old and very, very wise and he answers questions. You have to get lost, they say, to find him. You creep along through the overhanging underbrush. Somehow he knows you're coming to see him. And sure enough, you're going to see him, for suddenly—BAM! There he is. You ask, he answers. Downright uplifting!"

Medley clapped her hands. "Will you go and ask

him what he picks for Delicious?" she said to Gaylen.

"That's a good idea," said the Mayor, chuckling.

"The King did tell me I was to ask everybody," said Gaylen. "Do you think I could find him, Medley?"

"Oh, yes! It's easy!" she said eagerly. "I found him all by myself last summer and I wasn't even looking for him."

"Here there, Medley, you mustn't tell stories," said the Mayor, still chuckling.

"But I *did*, Papa!" she insisted. "That day when we were playing hide-and-seek and I went too far into the forest. Don't you remember? I saw the woldweller while I was lost. He had a rabbit tied to his belt and he was climbing up a tree."

The Mayor stopped chuckling. "Medley," he said severely, "you know very well that a woldweller is just something in a story. Nobody lives for hundreds of years up in a tree! We'll have to stop telling fairytales if you're going to start believing them." And he sent her off to bed.

"Children get ideas into their heads sometimes," said

the Mayor when Medley was gone. He lit his pipe and settled back in his chair. "Of course, you're only a child yourself, really."

"Oh, no," Gaylen protested. "I'm twelve years old."

"Oh," said the Mayor. He puffed away at his pipe and then he said, "There was a time, I understand, when people really believed in things like woldwellers and dwarfs and the rest. Very little insight in their outlook. But of course we're much too advanced for that sort of thing these days. We've overcome the underlying superstitions." And he blew a smoke ring and looked very pleased with himself.

"It's true, just the same," said Medley to Gaylen the next morning. "I saw that woldweller just as clear as clear."

"If he's really there, he'll have to be found and registered," said Gaylen. "I have to go through the forest anyway to get to the next town. I'll look for him."

"Come back some day," whispered Medley close

to his ear so that her father wouldn't hear, "and tell me what he chose for Delicious."

When Gaylen was ready to leave, the Mayor took him aside for a moment. "See here," he said seriously. "If I were you, I'd be on the lookout for this fellow who's going about talking against the King. I don't know who he is, but I was told he rides a big gray horse and looks very troublesome."

But Gaylen knew at once. The stranger on the big gray horse was Hemlock.

Gaylen rode out of the town soon after, into a morning that was hung with clouds and threatened rain. No one said goodbye except the Mayor and Medley. A few of the townspeople were gathered at the well, standing about in silence. But as Gaylen and Marrow clopped by, one old man with a little pig under his arm leaped up and screeched, "HAM!" The horse shied sideways in surprise and bounded off across the square. When he was calmed again to a walk, Gaylen turned around for a last look. He saw that two of the women were trying to dump the old man into the well, while a third had hold of his arm and was trying to pull him out again. None of them looked as if they were enjoying it. And the little pig stood squealing on the cobblestones.

HE FOREST TOWARD WHICH Gaylen turned his horse rose green and silent just across the meadows beyond the town. He was halfway there and wondering how soon the rain would begin when, with a great flapping and squawking, the cockatoo dropped suddenly out of the heavy sky and landed on his shoulder in a graceless splash of feathers. It clung there, rocking dizzily for a moment, and Gaylen found breath enough to gasp, "For the love of Hector . . . !" before he remembered that it was Wednesday and time for news from the castle. He lifted the bird down from his shoulder and gently removed the folded paper tied to its leg. On the paper was written:

Everyone here keeping his temper pretty well. The King gave a party on Monday with a minstrel to sing, and to avoid arguments he made everyone bring his own supper in a basket. But there is something strange—Hemlock has disappeared altogether. We searched his rooms and found nothing but a note which said, "No use to search—there's nothing to find. Divide one by two and three will come to the fore." I don't like it. I am well and hope you are the same. *The P.M.*

As well as he could, what with holding on to the bird at the same time, Gaylen turned the paper over and wrote on the other side:

Have registered the first town. Everyone fought about it and there are no two votes alike. Hemlock is riding about talking against the King. Thank you, I am very well.

Vaungaylen

He tied the paper to the cockatoo's leg and she flew off with a relieved squawk. Gaylen sat watching her disappear into the dark clouds that were nudging each other down the sky. "I wonder what Hemlock is trying to do," he said to himself. "It can't be simply that he's angry at the King for not having nuts at dinner." But he urged Marrow forward out of a clump of clover and turned again to his mission.

By the time he had reached the first oaks and beeches of the forest and was passing in among them, the rain had begun to fall. It splopped and plipped on the leaves over his head, while here and there occasional drops that found their way down through the branches fell like small stars to hang trembling in his hair or the horse's mane. But the deeper he went into the forest, the thicker became the roof of leaves over his head, and even though he could hear the first growls of thunder promising a heavy storm, he stayed dry as the grass on the forest floor. There were low branches now, waiting to catch at his hair if he kept his high perch, so he climbed down from the saddle and he and Marrow went side by side in a very companionable manner, listening to the rain. Gaylen was not at all worried about losing his way, in spite of the fact that there was no path, and he had stopped worrying about Hemlock. As a matter of fact, he was thinking about the woldweller.

There was a lovely greenish glow in the forest, a glow pierced everywhere by tree trunks like fingers thrust into an aquarium full of tinted water; and Gaylen slipped between them like a small fish. With the trees all around him and the rain dancing on the leaves high over his head, he felt as if he were going deeper and deeper into a world that existed tranquil and quite separate from the one he had left behind. He had just decided that the woldweller must surely be real when he came smack up against the most enormous tree trunk of all and a voice croaked down at him from somewhere overhead:

"Stop where you are, boy, and look around! You've

stumbled right into the exact and precise center of the forest and that doesn't happen once in a hundred years."

G AYLEN WAS NOT SURPRISED at all when he heard the voice. He tied his horse to a nearby sapling and stood looking up at the branches of the huge oak. He couldn't see anything but a dense mass of leaves. After a moment the leaves trembled and the voice called, "Stand back! I'm coming down." The end of a long, frayed rope appeared and dropped to the ground. There was another, wilder disturbance among the leaves and at last a figure emerged, climbing cautiously down the rope.

The woldweller was a very, very old man. He was wrapped in rough cloth that exactly matched the bark of the tree, and about his waist, hung from a twiny sort of belt, were a number of objects—a saucepan, a wooden fork, and various other things—which clanked and rattled as he descended. His hair hung gray and tangled and so long that, as he came lower, Gaylen saw it was his hair he had tied about his middle for a belt, not a piece of twine at all.

"You're the woldweller!" said Gaylen.

The old man reached the ground and turned to look up at him. He was small and his face was as dry and wrinkled as a walnut shell. "I'm *a* woldweller. There's one in every forest, you know. I'm nine hundred years old," he said, and then added anxiously, "Do you believe that?"

"Yes, I do," said Gaylen, for the woldweller certainly looked as if he were nine hundred years old. His eyes were so hung about with wrinkles and folds that they looked like two bright little pins pressed into a prune.

"That's right," said the woldweller with satisfaction.

"I *am* nine hundred years old. And you came looking for me to ask me questions. Nobody does that any more, except him. They used to come all the time, two or three hundred years ago, but they don't believe in me any more."

"There's a little girl in the town who believes in you," said Gaylen. "She told me that she saw you here last summer."

"Yes, yes, that's so. Some of the children still believe. But they don't come to look for me. Their mothers and fathers won't let them, you know. They don't believe in me but at the same time they're afraid I might be true, so they won't let their children come. Curious." The woldweller sat down and stared off through the trees. He was so dry and light that the leaves under him lay quite crisp and uncrushed. "Of course, I've plenty to do without answering questions," he said after a moment. "There's the forest to look after. I hope you didn't break off any branches on your way in. Careless, heedless, thoughtless you are, all of you. No appreciation. It was always like that, even in the old days." The woldweller opened his mouth wide and wailed, a mournful wail of chagrin that seemed to wrap itself around the tree trunks and hover like smoke before it drifted away. He sat scowling for a moment and then turned abruptly to Gaylen. "Can you climb a rope, boy?"

"I guess so," said Gaylen.

"Come up, then, and I'll show you something." The woldweller scurried up the rope and disappeared. Gaylen climbed after him, puffing and straining, and managed at last to poke his head through the first tier of leaves. He looked up. The rope still stretched far away above him, threading among branches that reached out in every direction like thick, muscled arms in frothy green sleeves.

"Come on, boy, climb!" came the woldweller's voice high over his head.

Up and up went Gaylen, resting when a convenient branch presented itself, until at last he came to the end of the rope where it was knotted firmly around a sturdy branch. Here, more than halfway up the huge tree, was a hole in the trunk and out of this hole the woldweller peered beadily.

"Come in, boy. Come in. You're slow as a caterpillar." Gaylen dropped feet first through the hole and found himself in a neat round room completely empty except for a pile of ashes in the center and a mattress of leaves against the wall. On the other side there was another, larger hole and toward this the woldweller gestured impatiently. "Over here, boy," he said. "Never mind the room. Look over here."

Gaylen crossed and looked out through a wide break in the leaves.

"What do you see, boy?" asked the woldweller.

"Rain," said Gaylen. "Rain and treetops. Like a wet, bumpy green floor!"

"What else?" prodded the woldweller.

"I can see a little of the first town, too," said Gaylen, trying not to feel dizzy. "Way over there. It looks so small!"

"That's right," crowed the woldweller. "It *is* small. And flimsy. You've got nothing that lasts, you know. That's not the first town that ever stood there. There was one before that, and one before *that* one, on back for nine hundred years. But this tree has stood here all along. What do you make of that, boy?"

"I think," said Gaylen, feeling his head begin to spin, "that I'd like to go back down now."

The woldweller stared at him for a moment, an expression of disgust deepening the wrinkles around his mouth. Then he sighed. "No change," he said. "Not in nine hundred years. Not," he added, "that it matters. Very well. Let's go down."

WHEN THEY HAD REACHED the ground again and Gaylen was feeling better, he sat and watched the woldweller curiously. The old man was pacing about, examining the bark on nearby tree trunks for grubs, and patting down dead leaves around the roots of saplings that thrust up here and there. He was as tender in his ministrations as a mother with a baby.

"What sort of questions did the people bring, the ones who came to see you in the old days?" Gaylen asked after a while.

"Oh, they wanted to know about love, you see," answered the woldweller, disappearing behind a thick trunk. "War, too," he added, emerging on the other side. "And power. How to gain power. Things of that sort. A lot of nonsense. But I knew the answers then and I do now. *He* still comes, of course. At least he asks a few unusual questions."

"Who comes?"

"Why, he lives in the castle of the present King. He calls himself Hemlock."

Gaylen drew in his breath sharply. So Hemlock knew about the woldweller and came to see him! The shivery feeling spread over him again. "What does Hemlock want to know when he comes?"

The woldweller sat down on a tree root and yawned. "He used to come here when he was a little boy. I taught him magic tricks and he brought me rabbits." He rattled the wooden fork against the saucepan and licked his lips. "He still brings me rabbits. I had one yesterday. He's a bad man, you know. Evil. But it's nothing to me. He can be evil if he chooses. He's a *man*, after all. Men have had wars before and will again."

"Wars!" said Gaylen. "Is that what he wants? War? But why?"

"Power, of course," said the woldweller indifferently. "Power, just as it was in the old days and just as it always will be. I'll help him as long as he brings me rabbits. Why not? It's nothing to me."

"But how do you help him?" asked Gaylen. "What does he want to know when he comes here? Please, you must tell me!"

"No, I mustn't," said the woldweller, "but I will. Why not? He wants advice, that's what he wants. I give him advice. I'm a woldweller and this forest belongs to me and I can answer any question he asks." He opened his mouth and wailed again, but this time it was a wail of pride and satisfaction that split the glimmering green calm of the forest like an ax. Then his voice dropped and he whispered, "He wants to know how to find the dwarfs who made the whistle, and he wants to know how to find Ardis in the lake . . ."

A sudden whinny from Marrow interrupted him. The horse lifted his head to listen and his nostrils flared. Then Gaylen heard it too—someone was coming through the trees.

"STOP!" boomed a voice, and Hemlock himself appeared, striding toward them. He was leading his great gray horse, Ballywrack, who was breathing hard, as if he had just been ridden far and fast. Hemlock's face was as angry as the thunder that still muttered far above the trees. He came and stood over them, his fists clenched at his sides. "One more word to this meddling child," he said to the woldweller, "and there will be no more rabbits for another hundred years!"

Gaylen drew back against the tree trunk, but the woldweller only yawned again and scratched his head.

"Have you got a rabbit for me now?" he asked. Hemlock produced a rabbit from under his cape and held it out. The woldweller took it and tied it to the belt of hair at his waist. "I've seen it all," he said quietly and his eyes went vague and cloudy. "Around and around. Coming and going like the spokes of a wheel for hundreds of years. It's nothing to me." He scuttled up the rope, disappearing into the leaves overhead and pulling the rope up after him. "Stop and look around you, boy," his wheezy voice called faintly from somewhere far above. "You're in the exact and precise center of the forest and that doesn't happen *twice* in a hundred years."

Gaylen stood looking up for a moment and then he turned to Hemlock. Suddenly he felt very young and skinny. "He means I'll never see him again, doesn't he?"

Hemlock scowled at him. "Take your horse and go on with your poll, or I'll tell the King you've been mooning about the countryside wasting his time. I don't know what the old man told you but it doesn't really matter. The King wouldn't believe you anyway.

He'd think you were mad if you went to him with tales about a woldweller."

Gaylen untied Marrow and started to walk off. Then he gathered all his courage and turned around. "Who is Ardis?" he asked. "The woldweller said you were looking for Ardis in the lake."

"He told you that, did he?" said Hemlock. "Well, it doesn't matter. Ardis is only a dream." He drew his cape more closely about him and scowled again. Then he shrugged and added, "What good are dreams, after all?" He turned and strode away, with Ballywrack after him, and disappeared among the trees. The green light of the forest glimmered tranquil and silent once more and Gaylen was left alone.

He trudged off, leading his horse, and it was several minutes before he remembered that he hadn't asked the woldweller about his favorite food. But it seemed fair to guess that he preferred rabbits over everything else. Gaylen took out the large notebook and wrote:

Name – Woldweller
Age – Nine hundred years
Home – The exact and precise center of the forest
Choice for Delicious – Rabbits

And then he put away the notebook and continued on his way out of the forest.

HE RAIN HAD STOPPED when Gaylen came at last to the end of the forest, and the sun, dropping away behind the mountains, bled orange and pink over the last remaining clouds. He remembered that he had had nothing to eat since breakfast, and now, as he rode along, he looked about for a friendly clump of trees where he could eat his supper and sleep for the night.

A small orchard beside a stream some distance away looked cozy enough and he turned his horse toward it gratefully.

As he came nearer, he heard singing and saw the red wink of a campfire. Someone else had found the orchard appealing, but perhaps, thought Gaylen, whoever it was wouldn't mind sharing a tree or two. He rode closer and found that he could make out the words of the song:

Heigh road, high road,
All roads are my road.
*   Where, whither, whence when the wind cries "Go"?*
Heigh way, high way,
All ways are my way.
*   Here, hither, hence when the wind lies low.*

Sweet moon, old moon,
You and me are bold, moon.
*   Rise after lunch when the sun's on high.*
Sweet light, bright light,
Stay for a night light.
*   Lie, linger, laugh when the sun's gone by!*

Gaylen climbed down from Marrow's back and left him to browse in the sedges beside the stream. Tossing the saddlebag across his shoulder, he made his way through the trees to where the campfire crackled. A young man was sitting cross-legged against a tree trunk, turning a spitted chicken over the flames. He wore a suit of red and yellow and there was a lute lying beside him, a splash of brightly colored ribbons tied to its neck with their long ends splayed out over the grass like a rumpled rainbow. A dog lay nearby, a big brown dog who wagged his tail and barked when he saw Gaylen coming toward the fire.

"Hello, boy," said the young man, looking up. "Sit and have a bit of supper. The chicken's nearly done."

"Thank you!" said Gaylen. "And would it be all right if I spent the night here, too?"

"Why, of course it's all right! It isn't *my* orchard, you know. It belongs to everybody. Or if it doesn't, it should. In any case, I'll be glad for the company."

"I have some apples here," said Gaylen, putting down his saddlebag. He found that he was feeling very glad for the company himself. "Some apples, and some cold fried fish. Share and share alike."

All in all, it was a good and happy supper, and

the brown dog cleaned up the scraps. There were no more walnuts in the apples, either, which was a great relief to Gaylen.

"Now then," said the young man, "we can talk. Talking is almost as good as singing. My name is Canto and this brown beast here is my dear friend Muzzle. We've come across the mountains to the west and we're headed over the mountains to the east. We sing for kings and anybody else who'll stop to listen."

"It must be fine to travel about," said Gaylen. "I've never been anywhere before. I've lived in the castle here all my life and this is my first trip. My name is Vaungaylen."

"Well, now," said the young man, "if you've lived in the castle here, maybe you can tell me something about it. I stopped there two days ago and there was a very strange party in the evening. Everyone brought his own supper in a basket and nobody smiled at anybody. I started to sing a funny song I know about a cook and a Christmas pudding, but the King made me stop and sing something else!"

So Gaylen told the story of the Prime Minister's

dictionary and of how he himself was off on a poll to settle the dispute. The minstrel listened with such interest that Gaylen went on to tell him about Hemlock and the woldweller. But the minstrel put back his head and laughed. "Well now, as to *that*," he said, "I wouldn't have believed that. Any old man may live up in a tree and claim to be a woldweller, but that doesn't mean it's true."

"But it was all just like the legend," said Gaylen thoughtfully.

"Oh, well, there are legends, to be sure—I sing about them all the time. But they're only pretty stories just the same."

It was true, thought Gaylen to himself, that the spell of the forest and the woldweller was beginning to fade as the daylight faded, and Hemlock seemed far away and harmless. What damage could he do, after all, with woldwellers and dwarfs? But still, there was a walnut in the apple, and the Prime Minister was worried, and—he yawned. He was getting very sleepy.

"Did you ever hear of someone called Ardis?"

he asked at last, remembering. "Ardis in the lake?"

"Now *there's* a pretty song," said the minstrel, taking up the lute and running his thumb over the strings. "A sad and pretty song, most of it forgotten. I'll sing you the part my father taught to me, the only part he learned from *his* father. There must have been much more of it once, but it's been lost, you see, for hundreds of years."

Gaylen stretched himself out on the grass as the minstrel plucked from the lute a sweet cluster of chords. The night breeze stirred the gay ribbons and fanned the last twigs in the campfire into fresh low flame. Muzzle yawned and closed his eyes, and the minstrel began to sing:

> *Two moons wander where the water curls,*
> *Two white moons in a pair of skies—*
> *Two moons yonder like a pair of pearls*
> *There by the lake where the water swirls,*
> *There where she sits with her wet green eyes,*
> *There where she weeps and droops and sighs,*
> *Poor Ardis where the water curls.*
>
> *Wet stars shimmer in the mermaid's tears,*
> *Wet white stars on the sky's dark sleeve—*

Wet stars glimmer through the long dark years,
Call down the words that she never hears,
Call to her there where the waters heave,
Call to her, "Ardis! Why do you grieve?"
No answer but the mermaid's tears.

Gaylen fell asleep as the last notes dropped from
the lute and melted on the warm night air like snow-
flakes. And his dreams were full of lakes and rain and
the gleam of the mermaid's scales among the reeds.

IN THE MORNING, MUZZLE
was the first to wake up, and
since his usual way of starting a new day was to go

about licking the faces of anybody who happened still to be sleeping, it was no time at all before Gaylen and Canto were up themselves and about the business of breakfast.

An apple apiece and a leg of cold chicken from last night's supper did the job nicely.

"There'll be apples on these trees in a few weeks," remarked the minstrel, looking up at the branches overhead, where the first buds were fattening toward their sweet annual explosion into white. There was a bluejay nagging among the leaves, his proud feathers an exact match to the morning sky. Gaylen sat, too, looking up contentedly. The Prime Minister had predicted that spring would escape notice this year, but nonsense! How could such a thing be? It was impossible this morning to believe in anything disagreeable or threatening. Still, thinking of the Prime Minister made him remember why he was sitting here, miles from the castle, on an early April morning. There was a poll to be completed, after all, he told himself sternly.

"I have to register your choice for Delicious," he said to the minstrel. He brought out the large note-book and sat poised to write.

"But I don't belong to your kingdom," said Canto.

"I know," said Gaylen, "but you don't especially belong to any other, either, so I think I should write you down. You might decide to settle here."

"I'll never settle anywhere," said Canto, "but you can write me down if you like. I've an easy choice for Delicious, but not a simple one. Are you ready? The most delicious thing of all is a cold leg of chicken eaten in an orchard early in the morning in April when you have a friend to share it with and a brown dog to clean up the scraps. You'll have to write it all down because every word is important."

Gaylen wrote carefully in the notebook and then he said, "I have to know your age. And what shall I put for your home?"

"My age is twenty-five, I think," said Canto, "and my home is wherever you like. I'm intrigued by this poll of yours," he went on, "because it seems to me to be an excellent subject for a song. I'll come back some day and you can tell me how it all turned out. I'll come back when *you're* twenty-five."

"That's a long time from now," said Gaylen. "How will we know each other?"

"Here's an idea," said the minstrel, and he pulled out from the neck of his tunic a chain on which was hung a small key carved out of plain gray stone. "This key doesn't open any doors," he said, "and it doesn't close any coffers. My grandfather gave it to me years ago. He got it from *his* grandfather. He said it was a good-luck charm. Well, I've never had any luck to speak of, good or bad. But maybe it will do something for you. And then, you see, I'll come along when you're twenty-five and you can show it to me and I'll know it's you. You'll be able to recognize me all right because I'll still be a minstrel, only I'll be an old minstrel, almost forty, with a long gray beard and a shabby lute."

Gaylen took the chain and hung it around his neck and the key lay warm against his chest.

"That's right," said the minstrel. "Goodbye then, boy."

He whistled to the dog and the two strolled off, heading eastward where the sun was stepping high and golden above the mountains. As he went, the minstrel lifted the lute and sang into the clear morning air:

> *The way is long and high and hot.*
> *Be gay and sing! You may as well*
> *Be feeling light of heart as not.*
> *The way is long and high and hot,*
> *But mime the birds and praise your lot.*
> *Sweet freedom is the tale to tell.*
> *The way is long and high and hot.*
> *Be gay and sing! You may as well.*

Gaylen stood smiling after him, fingering the key on his chest. Then, with a sigh, he took up the saddlebag and went to fetch Marrow from the stream at the edge of the orchard. After frowning at his map for a moment, he turned the horse southwest toward the next town and started off again on the search for Delicious.

THE SECOND OF THE FOUR towns lay a good many miles ahead, but it was not a straight ride through, for there were three farms along the way and the farmers and their families all had to be polled. Gaylen had not gone far before he came upon a group of cows chewing calmly in a sunny meadow beside the road. Just beyond, a row of poplars stood guard over a small farmhouse and its attendant barn, coops, and sty. There was a woman sitting on the porch of the house, and out behind, in a tidy field, a man and a large ox were plowing the rich soil. Gaylen rode up to the house and called, "Gather round! Gather round! I'm here on the King's business!"

The woman on the porch peered out at the boy and the big horse in his royal draperies, and her eyes opened very wide. She put aside the bowl of potatoes she had been peeling and called in a loud voice, "Mildew! *Mildew!* Come here at once!" Then she came down the path. She was a big woman with a red face and red hands and she wore a dark jacket and a great many skirts and petticoats. The man who had been plowing loped puffing to her side and they both stood staring up at Gaylen with their mouths open.

Gaylen took out the proclamation and unrolled it, fumbling self-consciously. He read in a voice somewhat louder than necessary:

Let it be known that every single creature in my kingdom who is capable of speech shall register with my messenger the following information: name, age, home, and the food he or she honestly believes to be the most delicious of all foods.

Then he rolled up the proclamation again and took out the notebook.

The farmer and his wife looked at each other and then looked back at Gaylen. An expression of self-satisfaction spread over the woman's red face and she reached up a hand to smooth the knot of hair at the back of her neck. "The most delicious food, is it?" she beamed. "Well, now, there's no trouble with that. My name is Whimsey Mildew and I'm fifty-nine, and I make the best fruitcake in the kingdom. It's by far the most delicious thing there is and I'm sure a great many people will agree with me." She stopped and looked expectantly at her husband.

But the farmer scratched at his knee nervously and kept his eyes on Gaylen. "Did the King say we have to be honest?"

"Absolutely," said Gaylen.

"Honest, eh?" said the farmer. He looked miserably up at the sky and swallowed. Then he looked at Gaylen again. His eyes narrowed. He shoved his hands into his pockets and drew a deep breath. "My name is Mildew," he said slowly, "and I'm sixty-one, and *I just hate fruitcake!*" His wife's jaw dropped and she stared at him, her face changing to a deeper shade of red. "I don't care, Whimsey!" he cried. "I'm glad it's out at last. For thirty years I've been eating that fruitcake of yours—*ugh!*—when all I really wanted was a simple plumcake. *Plumcake!* Do you hear?"

"Plumcake?" choked his wife, her face now quite purple. "You'd rather have a soggy plumcake than my fruitcake? I can't believe it. I can't *stand* it! *Plumcake!*"

"Now, Whimsey, don't be cross," pleaded the farmer, but it was too late. She turned on him and grabbed at his jacket. He dodged away and headed off across the yard and out into the field, the plowed earth flying up from his heels, and his wife churned after him, mighty in anger, with her skirts flapping out behind.

Gaylen sat in dismay and watched them disappear into an alder wood behind the farm. He sat until he could no longer hear them shouting. And then all of a sudden he felt very tired. "No wonder the woldweller says there will always be wars," he said to Marrow. He wished he were back in the orchard again, listening to the minstrel's songs. But the minstrel was far away. Gaylen wrote the votes in the notebook and slid it into his saddlebag. Then he touched his horse's ribs with his heel and they moved slowly off down the road.

GAYLEN CAME TO THE NEXT farm when the sun stood high overhead. There were two little children playing under a tree in the yard, a wild pear tree just going pink with blossoms. When the children noticed Gaylen riding up, the little boy shouted, "Mother! Mother! Here's a big horse come in a pretty dress!" Their mother appeared in the doorway of the farmhouse and looked out. When she saw the horse, she drew back a little, shyly, but when she noticed how young the rider was, she took heart and stepped forward.

"Good day, sir," she said politely. "We're just about to have our midday meal. Will you come and join us?"

They gathered around the table with the farmer himself at the head, dishing out steaming bowls of stew. But when Gaylen read the proclamation, a shadow crossed the farmer's sunburned face.

"I was afraid you were the one," he said. "I've heard there's trouble in the kingdom. Why does the King want war?"

"But he doesn't!" said Gaylen. "All he wants is opinions." And he told them about the Prime Minister's dictionary.

"Just the same," said the farmer, setting his mouth,

"first comes a stranger in the night, riding up and banging on the door. He pushes in and shouts that there's trouble coming, that the kingdom is dividing against itself and that the King is trying to deceive us by sending around a messenger with just the kind of talk you've given us. He claims the King wants to set down laws about eating, laws that say we can have some things but not others. And now *you* come, just as he said you would."

"Hush!" said his wife. "He's only a boy!"

The farmer turned away from her angrily. "I don't want a war," he cried to Gaylen, "but, on the other hand, I grow vegetables on my farm. What if the King says no more vegetables? No one will buy my carrots and beans and my farm will be ruined, while my neighbor Mildew up the road grows fat from his wheat and barley."

Hemlock had done his work well. Gaylen saw that it would be useless to protest. "I have to register you anyway," he said. "I'm sorry."

The farmer and his wife and daughter voted stoutly for vegetables. The little boy said sweets at first, but his father spoke to him so sharply that he changed his mind.

Gaylen thanked them for the meal and rode away. He rode until dusk and then stopped at the last farmhouse, weary and hungry and hoping that a friendly soul inside would take him in for the night. He had ridden all through a glorious afternoon, but with such a heavy heart that he had not noticed the yellow primroses starring the grass along the way or heard the sweet song of linnets in the trees.

AYLEN CLIMBED DOWN from Marrow's back and tied him to a young sycamore in front of the little house. Then he took his saddlebag and went to the door. At first there was no response to his knocking, and then a voice called sharply, "Who is it then?"

"It's the King's messenger," he replied. "I've come on the King's business."

"Oh," said the voice. Then, "You don't say so! Well, all right. I'm coming." The door opened and a rosy, wrinkled face appeared, framed by the starched white ruffle of a mobcap. A smile spread over the face and the door opened wide. "Why, you're only a child!" said the old woman to whom the rosy face belonged. "Come in, child, and rest. Supper's on."

Gaylen stepped into a small, warm room. A pot of something lovely hung over the coals in a large fireplace, and against the wall a table was neatly laid for one. Bowls of white and pinkish haw stood everywhere. Gaylen sank onto a stool by the fire and peered into the pot, where, he now discovered, a rich soup of potatoes and onions rolled and bubbled.

"Go and wash up, child," said the old woman, "and we'll have some supper." She pointed to a corner of the room where a basin and pitcher stood on a low cupboard. Gaylen poured water from the pitcher into the basin and washed his dusty hands and face. He was feeling much better already. He dried himself with a bit of fluffy cloth that was folded beside the basin, and turned to the table, where the old woman was laying out another bowl and cup. She looked at him and said severely, "Let me see your hands." He held them out. "Very nice," she said at last, after turning them over to make sure both sides were clean. "Now, sit down." He sat and she filled his bowl with hot soup and put a spoon into his hand. Then she lit a fat candle that stood on the table, filled her own bowl, and sat, settling her skirts on the stool and clucking a little to herself like a pleasant old hen. They ate for a while in silence and then she put down her spoon and looked at him.

"So you're the King's messenger!" she said.

"Yes. I am," answered Gaylen.

"You don't say so!" she said, peering at him closely in the candlelight. She picked up her spoon and then put it down again. "I expect your old grandmother is very proud of you—such a child and such an important job," she said.

"I don't have an old grandmother," said Gaylen. "I don't have a mother, either. I'm an orphan, you see."

After a moment the old woman reached out a wrinkled hand and patted his arm. "You don't say so," she said gently.

They ate again, while Gaylen wondered to himself about mothers and grandmothers. He had never thought much about them, because the Prime Minister had given him as much love and attention as any child could want. But just the same it was curiously soothing, sitting here with this kind old woman. He felt a warmth in his bones that the soup alone could not account for.

"I'm sorry I didn't let you in right away, child," said the old woman when they had finished their supper. "But there was such a noise here last night. A very disagreeable stranger came to my door. I had to get Maunder to drive him away. And I thought you must be he coming back to try again."

She shook her head and frowned at the memory.

Hemlock, thought Gaylen. Then he asked, "Who is Maunder?"

"Why, that's Maunder over there," said the old woman, pointing to the corner by the fireplace. And there on a perch sat a large black crow. The crow had been sitting so still that Gaylen had not noticed it at all. But now, when he turned to look at it, the crow blinked its eyes rapidly and shook its feathers.

"Hello, child!" it rasped. "Hello, hello, hello! Whistles and keys! Whistles and keys!"

"Go over and say how-de-do to her while I clear up the table," suggested the old woman.

Gaylen went over to the corner and stood sleepily admiring the crow's shiny black feathers. "Hello, Maunder," he said, yawning. The crow cocked its head to one side and rocked for a moment on its perch. Then it looked him straight in the eye and said something so surprising that Gaylen was wide awake again instantly.

"Whistles and keys! Whistles and keys!" said the crow. "Poor Ardis lost her doll!"

AYLEN STOOD GAPING AT the bird, who had thrust its head under its wing and was pecking at itself fiercely. Ardis! Here was her name again, from a most unlikely source.

"Tell me about Ardis," he said to the crow eagerly. "Tell me something more!"

The crow settled its feathers and stared off in another direction. Then it cocked its head again and said, "Too bad! Too bad! Poor Ardis. Whistles and keys!" Then it turned itself around, with its back to Gaylen, and refused to say another word.

Gaylen went and stood by the fire, thinking. The old woman had rinsed and dried the dishes and was putting them away on a shelf. He watched her for a moment and then he said, "Where did you get that crow?"

"Why, my old man gave her to me long ago. He brought her down out of the mountains and gave her to me. She's very, very old."

"Does she always talk about Ardis?" asked Gaylen.

"Dear me, no," said the old woman, bringing a stool over to the fire and settling herself on it comfortably. "I've heard her mention the name a time or two. Not often. Once, I remember, a fishmonger came to the door and I bought a pretty trout for supper and Maunder kept me awake all night saying those same words she just said to you. But you don't have a fish with you anywhere that I can see. Still, there must be something that started her remembering."

"Poor Ardis!" croaked the bird to the corner. "Too bad. Too bad. Whistles and keys!"

"Why, that's it!" exclaimed the old woman suddenly. "It's that strange little key you're wearing round your neck, child. That's what must have reminded her!"

Gaylen lifted the key and looked at it. He had almost forgotten it was there. "This key doesn't have anything to do with Ardis," he said, turning it over in his hand. "Ardis is a mermaid. I heard about her in a song."

"Well, perhaps Maunder heard the same song once."

"But there's nothing about keys in the song," protested Gaylen. "At least, not in the part I heard." And then he sat down on the floor before the fire and told the old woman the whole story from the very beginning. When he got to the part about the woldweller, she folded her lips and clucked doubtfully, but when he told of his fears about Hemlock and the possible war to come, she shook her head and sighed.

"It's a heavy load you carry, child. A very heavy load," she said. "I wish I could help you, but I'm just an old woman. You must be very wise, living with the King as you do and knowing how to read and write. No doubt you'll find a way out of all your troubles. But come to bed now and sleep. For all your wisdom, you're still a child and you need your rest."

She tucked him away under an old quilt on a mattress which she spread out before the fire. And then she took the candle and went off to her own tiny bedroom behind the fireplace. But before she went she bent and smoothed his hair. "Good night, child," she said softly. "Sleep and dream."

And Gaylen slept as blissfully as he would surely have slept in the house of the grandmother he had never known.

In the morning he tried again to wheedle something more from the crow, but it wouldn't talk to him at all. The old woman fixed him a lunch of bread and cheese and tucked it into his saddlebag, and he wrote her choice for Delicious in the notebook: potato soup. Her name, she said, was Mrs. Copse.

"Goodbye! Goodbye, Vaungaylen!" she called to him as he rode away. "Come back again, child, when you can."

And from the window the crow relented with a final squawk: "Whistles and keys! Whistles and keys! Goodbye!"

Gaylen's hand went to the key that hung on his chest. His thoughts as he jounced along turned to the minstrel and the song he had heard in the orchard:

> *Wet stars glimmer through the long dark years,*
> *Call down the words that she never hears.*
> *Call to her there where the waters heave,*
> *Call to her, "Ardis! Why do you grieve?"*

"Well, at least," he said to Marrow, "I've discovered one thing. If the crow is right, Ardis grieves because she's lost her doll. But I certainly wish I knew why it seems so important."

HEN GAYLEN RODE INTO the second town that afternoon, he knew immediately that Hemlock had been there first. The people on the streets glared at him as he rode by and he could hear them murmuring: "There he is now." "I told you he'd come, you dolt." "Be quiet now." "Yes, there's trouble enough already." "Don't look at him." "Quick, get the children off the street—there'll be fighting again now that he's come."

Gaylen rode on to the center of the town and found a small, angry group of citizens waiting for him. When they saw him coming, they shoved one of their number forward and someone said, "Go ahead, Veto. You're the Mayor."

"Gather round, gather round," said Gaylen uncertainly. "I've come on the King's business."

The man called Veto looked at his neighbors for encouragement and then turned to Gaylen. "We know why you're here," he said. "We were warned." A large number of people were collecting to listen. Their faces were dark with anger and worry. "We'll do our best to see that the King's wishes are carried out," said Veto. "But we want to say first that we're very unhappy about it." He came closer and his voice rose with passion. "The King is setting neighbor against neighbor with this proclamation! We've heard that the first town has split right down the middle and business has come to a standstill!"

"Yes, yes, that's what we were told!" cried some of the people. Others muttered and watched one another suspiciously.

"There's room in this kingdom for all kinds of good things to eat!" Veto went on, raising his hand for silence. "If the King tries to strike out certain foods, some of us will be ruined!"

"That's true!" cried an anxious voice from the crowd.

"Yes, but which?" called another, deeper voice. "Which shall be ruined and which shall prosper?"

Gaylen sat listening in dismay. "But that's nonsense!" he cried. "The King isn't trying to ruin anybody. All he wants to do is find out what people like best to eat. It's completely and entirely harmless!" But nobody would pay the least attention to what he was saying.

The Mayor turned to the crowd and raised his hand again. "We must list our choices with the King's messenger," he said to them. "It's the King's command. We must do it, and we'll do it in an orderly way. Form a line and let's get it over."

Gaylen tightened his knees against Marrow's sides to keep them from trembling, and the horse shifted his hoofs uneasily. Spreading the notebook open on the saddle, he began to write down votes as the people shuffled slowly past him, but his hand shook and the ink smeared again and again. Veto stood close by, speaking quietly to people in the line, and for a time things went smoothly. Then a big man dressed in white moved up to register.

"I'm Winnow, the miller," he said in a loud voice, turning to smirk at the crowd. "My choice is bread. Ha-ha! Bread, do you hear? The King will never ask anyone to do without bread. He can't ruin *me*, at any rate!"

Instantly the fragile peace was shattered and the line dissolved. Somebody grabbed the miller around the neck and threw him down, and with shouts and cries the people were on one another. Marrow whinnied and spun round in a circle and the ink bottle resting on the saddle went flying off to smash on the cobblestones.

"Save yourself, boy!" yelled the Mayor. "Ride! Ride!"

Gaylen jammed the notebook into the saddlebag and banged his heels against Marrow's ribs. The horse reared, spun again on his hind legs, and shot off through the mob, galloping, galloping away across the town and out into the countryside, with his ears flattened against his head and his mane flying. And Gaylen hung on with his arms wrapped tight around Marrow's neck, sobbing into the wind.

IT WAS DUSK WHEN MARrow stopped running. They had left the road far behind and had come instead to a stream at the foot of the mountains. The horse waded in, his sides heaving, and began to drink noisily. Gaylen slipped exhausted from the saddle and stood in the water, leaning against Marrow's hot flank. Then he stooped and pulled off his boots, tossing them to the bank. The current gurgled around his ankles and he dug his toes thankfully into cool mud, where here and there smooth pebbles glimmered in the fading light like coins in a wishing well. He stood for a long time and then he waded out, threw off his rumpled clothes and, running back to the middle of the stream, threw himself down with a splash. The key around his neck, shiny and mysterious in its new wetness, lifted and stirred a little as the current washed over his chest. Gaylen lay there and let the water finger through his hair and spill around his forehead and nose. He opened his mouth and it trickled in at the corners. He drank deeply in this backwards fashion and lay with the water lapping over his tired body until he felt soothed and clean. Then he waded to the bank and slapped his clothes against a tree trunk to clear out the dust, putting them on again afterwards without drying himself.

There was still a good bit of Mrs. Copse's bread and cheese in his saddlebag, and this he ate for his supper, stretched out on the bank to listen to the water. Marrow stood nearby, munching among the grasses. After a while the moon rose, and Gaylen watched its wavering reflection in the stream. Soon he was sound asleep.

In the morning he was as pleased to see the stream again as if there were a chance it might have wandered off during the night. He took two of the last few apples from his saddlebag and gave one of them to Marrow. The other he ate himself, sitting with his toes in the water. When he had finished, he pulled on his boots, climbed onto the saddle, and rode his horse to a field nearby to look about.

Marrow had brought him well away from the main road in their wild flight of the day before, but, studying the map, Gaylen discovered that they were not so far from their route as he had feared. In the distance the ground rose sharply into steep hills and then heaved higher to form the southernmost arc of the mountains which ringed the kingdom. Somewhere ahead among the lower hills stood the third town. Gaylen's heart drooped at the thought of it, but he had a mission, he said to himself. He would carry it through one way or another. He turned Marrow toward the hills and started off across the field.

He had not gone far when he heard a familiar squawk. Looking up, he saw a white dot in the sky. Of course! It was Saturday. A few moments later the cockatoo was panting on his shoulder and he was reading another letter from the castle:

Vaungaylen: Finish poll as fast as possible. All seems to be falling to pieces. We are told kingdom splitting, Crisps against Squashies and both against King. Hemlock sure to be in on it somehow. Watch out for him. Hurry home. The sooner vote is tallied and posted, the sooner trouble will be over. And please—be careful.

The P.M.

Gaylen sent the cockatoo back with an anxious reply:

Hemlock riding ahead of me telling the people lies about

the King. He's trying to start a war because he wants the kingdom for himself. I will be careful.

Vaungaylen

HEN THE COCKATOO HAD flown away again, Gaylen sat for a while thinking. Two more towns to register, and clearly the thing to do was to try to get to them before Hemlock did, in the hope that it was not too late already. That way he could spread his warning first and finish the poll more peacefully. But he would have to ride harder and longer than he had up to now. He patted the glossy side of Marrow's neck and said, "Here we go, friend. It's up to us." He dropped the key down inside his shirt to keep it safe. "If ever I needed a good-luck charm, it's now," he said to himself. Then he touched his heels to the horse's ribs.

The surest route seemed to lie along the base of the steep slopes, and soon they were cantering briskly through stony bracken past tumbled rocks and boulders where here and there blue bugles swayed. Overhead, brooding clouds hunched across the sun. The green peaks of the mountains went gray and patches of grass on the hillside bent under the cool breath of a fresh, low breeze.

But Gaylen was too preoccupied with the new urgency of his mission to feel the loneliness of the countryside. He did not even notice that it was beginning to rain. The third town still lay far ahead, somewhere among the hills, and bending low in the saddle, Gaylen urged Marrow forward ever faster. He felt that he and the horse had become one creature, tireless and fleet, rushing through the air on a wind of its own creation. They flew along smoothly for miles, and then, all of a sudden, they came to a patch of loose pebbles. The speeding horse slipped sideways, stumbled, and fell heavily. Gaylen went spinning out of the saddle and came crashing to the ground some distance away. He sat for a moment in a whirl of shock, but when his head cleared he stood up and found with relief that he was not really hurt. He ran back to where Marrow was scrambling upright, whinnying softly. The horse had not fared so well. His right front leg was shoeless, and lame.

For the first time Gaylen noticed the rain. He stood stroking the horse, wondering what to do next, while raindrops spilled down his cheeks like tears. Now they could never reach the third town before Hemlock. He gathered up the horse's reins and started off, Marrow limping painfully behind him. A jagged glare of lightning suddenly split the heavy sky and thunder rolled. "Come on," he said to the horse. "We've got to find some kind of shelter." And he peered at the steep hillside. Not too far up, a flat boulder jutted out over a dim hollow. A cave, thought Gaylen, and he turned off the road and carefully led the horse up among the slippery rocks.

When he reached the mouth of the cave and looked inside, Gaylen found that it was dry and warm and much larger than he had expected. It was a cavern, really, with a great, arched ceiling. There was room enough on its floor for twenty boys and horses. Around its walls, huge boulders thrust up like jagged teeth, and at the back a tunnel yawned away into darkness.

Gaylen led Marrow in and, turning, leaned against the smooth stone at the entrance and looked out at the rain-smoked land. Lightning flared again and thunder crashed. As the noise mumbled off across the sky, Gaylen heard a new sound and peered out through the downpour. The way along which he had come lay below, dotted now with gleaming pools, and soon, splashing along from the opposite direction, a dark shape appeared. As it came closer, Gaylen saw that it was a horse and rider and that they were turning up the hill toward the cave. Behind him, Marrow whinnied and stiffened. Gaylen looked closer. The horse stumbling up through the rocks was Ballywrack and the rider was Hemlock. Gaylen turned and seized Marrow's reins. He pulled the horse after him behind one of the boulders, and waited, his heart pounding. A few moments later, Ballywrack thundered in at the entrance, Hemlock urging him on, and the two went past, down the dark throat of the cave, till they were swallowed up in blackness.

GAYLEN SAT BEHIND THE boulder and frowned. Everywhere he went, it seemed, Hemlock came after or had already been, weaving in and out of his path like an ill-intentioned wasp. He waited until the clang and echo of Ballywrack's hoofbeats faded before he came out of the shadows. He wrapped the loop of Marrow's reins around a loose rock, gave the horse a pat of reassurance, and stole away to the tunnel to follow. Feeling his way, he crept into black darkness down a twisting corridor of cool, smooth stone. The corridor was dry and fragrant—it smelled, surprisingly, of apples, like the cellar of a well-kept farmhouse. After a while it seemed to straighten out and Gaylen could see a glow of light at the end. Voices reached his ears and he hurried nearer to listen.

"I must talk to all of you right away!" Hemlock's deep voice demanded.

"Can't," said a second, strange voice. "Bevel's down in the mine and Thwart went off to sleep. I'll talk to you. For a few minutes. Then I've got things to do. Lots of things to do."

"Very well," said Hemlock. "Then listen. I've got to have a whistle. A new whistle, just like the old one. A whistle for the spring house in the lake."

"A whistle, is it?" said the strange voice. A ringing laugh echoed up the corridor. "Well, my friend, the first whistle was very special. Bevel made it with a fine drill and afterward the drill fell into the forge and melted. He could never make another whistle. Goodbye."

"Wait!" cried Hemlock. "Don't go! You've got to help me. It's extremely important!"

"It's not at all important to me," said the strange voice, "and I've got things to do."

"Listen," said Hemlock. "I know about the first whistle being lost. The woldweller told me. But if you made the first one, you can make another. Then I can open the door to the spring house, and when she goes in to get her doll, I can lock her in. Only for a day or two, until the last piece falls into place. Then the kingdom will be mine. I'll bring you apples, Pitshaft. All the apples you want. Make me a new whistle!"

"Go away," said the strange voice wearily.

"Wait!" cried Hemlock. "All I want to do is make sure Ardis doesn't interfere with the last step. I didn't want to start so soon. My plans were not complete. But this proclamation of the King's has set the stage too well—I can't let my chance slip by. The people will be fighting any day and the war will wear them down and then I can . . ."

"Tra-la," interrupted the strange voice. "What do I care for your wars and kingdoms? We have things to do here, many things to do. Bevel couldn't make another whistle even if he wanted to. Not without the drill. And the drill melted in the forge. I've given you enough of my time already."

"Then I'll have to take my chances," said Hemlock. His voice was low and cold. "But if she interferes, it will be the worse for her. Nothing must go wrong now."

"Go away," the strange voice said again. "It's nothing to me, all this. People are so foolish. They waste their time. They waste their time even though they have so little of it. We have forever and yet we never waste a moment. Go away and let me get back to my work."

There was the sound of light footsteps and a heavy,

metal door clanged shut. And then there was silence.

Gaylen turned and made his way rapidly back up the tunnel. He could hear the hoofs of the gray horse Ballywrack clattering behind him. He raced toward the cave and slipped behind the boulder just in time to quiet Marrow's nervous whinny. An instant later Ballywrack appeared, with Hemlock stiff and angry in the saddle. They went out through the mouth of the cave. The hoofbeats mingled with the drip of the rain and died away in the distance.

AFTER HEMLOCK HAD DISappeared, Gaylen sat in the shadows close to Marrow and tried to piece together the things he had heard in the tunnel. Ardis, the doll, the lost whistle, and Hemlock's words: "Nothing must go wrong now." Gaylen chewed on a thumbnail and frowned. "Now, how am I to find out what he means to do," he said to himself, "with a lame and shoeless horse?"

He was so lost in his puzzle that he didn't hear footsteps padding up through the tunnel toward the cave. Then suddenly there was talking just beyond him on the other side of the boulder.

"Raining again. No mushrooms today." It was the same strange voice he had heard in the tunnel.

"No mushrooms today," echoed a second, higher voice. "What a shame! Well, we've plenty of roots still. Hear the thunder!"

"It's fine," said the first voice. "Just like the mines in the oldest days when we were all together."

Gaylen peeped cautiously around the boulder and saw three small figures standing at the mouth of the cave. They were dressed simply, in gray and brown, and wore heavy leather belts around their waists. One had a head of short, tangled white hair, one's hair was yellow, and the other was completely bald. Suddenly the white-haired figure put a hand on the bald one's arm and cried, "Hist, Pitshaft! What do I smell?" Gaylen ducked down behind the boulder. "I smell apples, Pitshaft! Apples!"

"Apples it is," the one called Pitshaft answered. "You're right, Bevel. No doubt they belong to that boy there, hiding behind that boulder with his horse. We'll go and speak to him."

So they had known he was there all along! Gaylen stepped out from behind the boulder, feeling very foolish.

He found himself looking into the ruddy faces of three small, sturdy men. Their gaze, out of eyes gray as slate, was calm.

"Have you got apples, boy?" asked Pitshaft.

"Yes—excuse me—I have a few in my saddlebag," answered Gaylen timidly. "I didn't mean to be hiding—I came in to get out of the storm, and my horse has lost a shoe, and ..."

"It doesn't matter," said Pitshaft. "How many apples do you have?"

"Three, I think."

The white-haired Bevel smiled. "I would have guessed three exactly." The third man sniffed and nodded his yellow head but said nothing.

"What can we do for you, boy, in exchange for your apples?" asked Pitshaft.

"I'll give them to you gladly," Gaylen said.

"Fair exchange only," said Pitshaft. "Did you say your horse had lost a shoe?"

"Yes, and he's lame, too."

"Well, then, we'll make him a new shoe while he rests his leg. A day or two at the most should do it," said Pitshaft. "Bring your horse and your apples and come along." Off went the three, back down the tunnel, and Gaylen followed, wide-eyed and unresisting, leading the limping Marrow behind him.

The room at the end of the tunnel was bright with the glow of many torches, and in the center stood a large brazier in which red coals throbbed with heat.

Next to the brazier were an anvil and a big stone crock of water, and there were a great many tools and scraps of metal lying about. The room was roughly oval in shape, and Gaylen, looking around, dropped Marrow's reins and gasped. The stone walls and ceiling were carved everywhere in low relief, carved so beautifully that Gaylen stood with his mouth hanging open in admiration.

There were forest scenes where the leaves of exquisite trees frothed low over all manner of animals busy among delicate weeds and grasses. There were underwater scenes with strange fish, tumbling waterfalls, and frondy plants on narrow stems. There were scenes which showed forges and mines far below the earth; and on the ceiling, clouds sailed before the wind across a starry sky and graceful birds dipped and wheeled. In the wavering light of the torches, the whole tableau seemed to breathe with motion and life. Here and there about the walls, benches and tables had been hewn out, and there were a number of arches, each fitted with a heavy metal door.

It was by far the most remarkable room Gaylen had ever seen. He turned round and round trying to look at all of it at once and as he turned he caught sight of what was surely the most amazing part of all. In a ledge opposite the entrance, a sort of basin had been carved. Over the basin curved the graceful body of a mermaid holding a water lily with fragile, pointed petals, and out of the center of the lily, in steady, measured rhythm, shining drops of water from some underground stream fell and splashed into the basin.

"Take your horse and go and drink," said Pitshaft. Gaylen drew Marrow across the room, and while the horse dipped into the water, he stood gazing up at the carving of the mermaid. She was very young, with a round, lovely face, and the hand holding the water lily had curling, graceful fingers. And he saw that in the other hand she held a little doll made of jointed stones with a bit of trailing fern for hair.

"Thwart carved her," said Pitshaft, pointing to the

silent little man with yellow hair. "He carved her long ago. She's Ardis."

GAYLEN STARED AND STARED at the mermaid. There seemed to be something marvelous hidden in the carving that he was seeing and yet not seeing—something extremely important. He bent to drink from the basin, straightened, and stared again, but whatever it was that was hidden there eluded him. He turned away and saw that Bevel was blowing up the coals in the brazier with a large bellows while Pitshaft, tongs in hand, held a rod of iron into the licking flames. When the iron was white-hot, Pitshaft laid it on the anvil and began to hammer. BONG bongity *ping* tap, BONG bongity *ping* tap—the hammer danced and the hot iron began to flatten. Into the flames again and out, and again the hammer rang, and the iron curved like a reluctant snake. Over and over, heat, hammer, heat, hammer, and bit by bit a perfect horseshoe was formed. Then, *hiss-ss-ss!* Pitshaft flung it into the crock of water. He turned and said abruptly, "Time for supper." All three dwarfs looked at Gaylen. He took the last three of the King's apples from his saddlebag and handed them round.

"Soup first," said Pitshaft. "Some for the boy too." Thwart went out through one of the arched doors and returned with a bubbling pot and four stone bowls. They sat all together at one of the carved tables and drank a strange but savory soup of tender roots in a salty broth. Then the three ate their apples, slowly and lovingly, stems, cores, and all.

Afterward, Pitshaft went around the room and put out most of the torches and then he disappeared through another of the arched doors. In a moment he came back carrying a sort of flute. He sat down on a bench across the now shadowed room and began to play. The voice of the flute was rich and woody and the tune was solemn. Bevel rose after a moment and began to dance, swaying and turning slowly and seriously. Thwart took out a pipe and tobacco and smoked peacefully in the dimness.

Gaylen sat wide-eyed. The carvings on the walls merged and trembled in the flickering light. From the quivering leaves of a tall tree he saw the wrinkled face of the woldweller peeping out at him, while above the basin the stone Ardis blinked happily and her scales sparkled. He looked from scene to scene and a question occurred to him.

"Why are there no people in the carvings?" he whispered to Thwart, who still sat smoking at the table.

When the dwarf answered, his voice was low and dreamy. "The waters belong to Ardis, the trees to the woldwellers, the skies to the wind. And the mountains belong to us."

"But what belongs to the people?" asked Gaylen.

Smoke curled around the dwarf's quiet face. "Nothing," he answered.

Gaylen tried to think about this but he was beginning to feel very fuzzy and peculiar. The fumes from Thwart's pipe filled his head like incense. The husky music of the flute, Bevel's weaving, sober figure, and the dappled, pulsing pictures on the walls seemed to blend and blur into a cone of sound and shadow. They began to revolve slowly before his eyes, to whirl and ebb and dim into blackness. His head dropped down on the table and he was asleep.

Gaylen half woke now and then, only to sleep again. The drip of the water into the basin measured his dreams and sometimes he thought he heard the bong of the hammer on the anvil, but these would dissolve into visions of dripping forests and the hollow clop of distant hoofbeats, and these, in turn, into the sobbing of the mermaid on a faraway bank.

When at last he woke completely, he felt new and fresh. The chamber was brightly lit with fresh torches, but it was empty except for Marrow, who munched dry grasses someone had piled for him near the carved basin. Gaylen ran to the horse and hugged him round the neck. He stooped to examine the lame leg. It seemed quite strong again and on the hoof was the bright new shoe. It was time to go.

Gaylen looked around and wondered where the dwarfs had gone. He decided that he needn't wait to say goodbye. They had had their apples and Marrow had his shoe. He gathered up the horse's reins and started for the tunnel. Then he turned for a last look at the stone mermaid. Suddenly, as he gazed, he saw what it was that had eluded him before. Behind the mermaid's arching body was another, larger shape on which she seemed to hang, her finny tail and one graceful arm curving around it. The other shape was all at once piercingly familiar. It was exactly like the one that hung inside Gaylen's tunic: a gray stone key. And there was a hole down through the middle, exactly—he now saw for the first time—like a whistle's. Above the mermaid, nearly hidden in the twisting branches of a spindle tree, sat a family of crows. And as he stared in amazement, a rasping voice scratched across his memory, a voice that had called after him in the morning sun of another day, "Whistles and keys! Whistles and keys! Goodbye!"

G AYLEN RODE MARROW up through the tunnel and out into the brilliance of a golden morning. His eyes squinted painfully after the dimness underground, but he was too stifled with excitement to notice. Here, then, hanging under his jerkin, was perhaps the very whistle Hemlock had wanted Pitshaft to replace, the very whistle lost for hundreds of years. How in the world the minstrel's family had come to possess it he could not even guess. He pulled it up out of his tunic and looked at it. Yes, there might once have been a hole down through the middle, but now it was clogged with centuries of grit.

Gaylen slid down from Marrow's back and broke a long, sharp thorn from a hawthorn tree. He sat on a rock and poked at the top of the key. A bit of the grit loosened. He shook it out and began to work in earnest, poking and scraping. After a time the hole was cleaned out and he sat looking at his treasure in wonder. The minstrel had said it didn't open any doors and yet somehow it must. Perhaps when it was blown, something magical happened. He put it to his lips and blew through the hole, but he could hear nothing—only the whoosh of his own breath rushing out through the other end. He looked about, but the rocky landscape remained unchanged. No puffs of green smoke, no boulders turning by themselves in their ancient hollows. Still, if Hemlock was so anxious to find it and if Ardis wept for it, it had to be very valuable. He would hurry through the polling of the last two towns, he told himself, and then he would go to Ardis and give it back to her. He climbed into the saddle and nudged Marrow into a canter, his thoughts full of the woldweller, the dwarfs, and the mermaid he had yet to find.

The country through which he jogged was slowly softening. Rocks on the hillsides began to give way to patchy grass and the trees were fuller and more frequent. Gaylen heard birds nesting noisily in the branches and once a fearful rabbit scalloped across his path. Then, as they rounded a shrubby hillock, Gaylen reined in hastily. A flock of lumpy sheep filled the way just ahead, baaing hugely as they crowded across and on up the hillside. A boy of about Gaylen's age strolled beside them. When he saw Gaylen, he stopped and stared rudely.

"Hey there," called Gaylen, "what's today?"

"Well, now," said the boy, furrowing his brow in mock concentration. "Riddles so early in the morning? I know the answer, though. Today is the day tomorrow becomes and yesterday used to be." He grinned wickedly.

"No, I meant what weekday is it," said Gaylen, frowning a little.

"But it's not a weak day at all," said the boy, raising his eyebrows in a good imitation of surprise. "I'd have called it a strong day with a sun like this."

"Look here," said Gaylen. "I only meant, is it Sunday or Monday or what?"

"Why didn't you say so, then?" said the boy. "I could have told you right away. It's Tuesday."

Tuesday! Gaylen forgot his annoyance for a moment. Then he had slept three nights in Pitshaft's cave. Hemlock would be far ahead by now. "Hey there," he said to the boy anxiously. "Have you seen any strangers on horseback along here?"

"Yes," said the boy. "You."

Gaylen swallowed his anger and tried again. "Have you seen a man ride by on a big gray horse? He would have been wearing a cape."

The boy scratched his head. "No," he said at last. "I'd have remembered a thing like that. You don't often see a horse wearing a cape."

"Now look here!" cried Gaylen. "I'm the King's messenger and I'm here on the King's business!"

"You're here on the King's horse, too," said the boy and his eyes narrowed. "I know who you are and

I know what you're doing. You can list my favorite food as mutton. I'm thirteen years old and I live a mile from here. My name is Decry and some day I shall be Prime Minister." He threw back his head and laughed loudly. "Tell that to the King if he's still king when the war is over."

"The war?" asked Gaylen quickly. "What do you know about the war?"

"My father and all his friends have gone to fight," answered the boy. "All of his enemies, too. We're Squashies. They're Crisps."

Gaylen took out the notebook and wrote while the boy watched him. Then he asked, "How long will it take me to get to the third town?"

"A very long time," said the boy.

"A very long time?" echoed Gaylen, discouraged.

"Well, yes, of course!" said the boy gleefully. "Your horse is standing still!"

Gaylen gave a shout of rage and dug his heels into Marrow's sides. The horse sprang forward, vaulted neatly over the last few straggling sheep, and bounded down the road. Gaylen looked back over his shoulder and saw the shepherd boy grinning after him. He turned around again hastily, his cheeks flaming, and pressed Marrow hard till, after an hour, the rooftops of the third town shone in the distance.

WHEN GAYLEN RODE UP TO the third town, he found the gate shut tight. He climbed down from the saddle and banged till his knuckles were sore. At last a head appeared above the gate. It was a woman with her hair tied up in a kerchief.

"Squashie or Crisp?" she barked down at him fiercely.

"Neither one," Gaylen answered. "I'm the King's messenger and I'm here on the King's business."

"It's him!" shrieked the woman, and instantly a great many other heads appeared above the gate, all women and all yelling at once: "He's the one!" "Warmonger!" "Husband killer!" "Food stealer!" "It's all your fault our men have gone away!" "Hit him! Hit him!" And they began pelting him with cabbages, tomatoes, and every other vegetable large enough to be thrown effectively.

Gaylen scrambled up on Marrow's back as fast as he could and galloped away from the walls of the town, the screams of the women fading behind him. He was rigid with anger. First the shepherd boy and now these women and their vegetables! His cheek smarted where an onion had banged into it. "I'll go away forever!" he cried to Marrow. "People are unbearable! They won't listen, except to lies, and they fight all the time *and I have had enough!*"

He turned the horse toward the hills and was soon riding up a steep grassy slope. He kept going, up and up past trees and rocks and shallow caves, till

Marrow, exhausted, spotted a clear little stream and refused to go beyond it. Gaylen slid out of the saddle and, leaving the horse to drink, went and sat on a smooth rock and scowled down at the land rolling away below like a map of itself.

"Unbearable!" His pride throbbed like a new bruise. "Why don't they send for me to come home?" he wondered. "They know how bad things are." He thought about the Prime Minister and his hurt deepened. "He knows I'm all alone out here and yet there he sits, safe in the castle, tinkering with that silly dictionary. He's probably forgotten all about me." A picture formed in his mind, in which the Prime Minister, basket in hand, tripped gaily as a girl about the palace garden, humming and picking flowers. He studied this picture with grim and bitter satisfaction. Then he stood up and thrust out his chin. "I'll take the whistle back to the mermaid," he said with decision, "and then I'll go and live with the dwarfs or the woldweller. *They* never quarrel or fight and they don't care about people any more than I do. To the devil with the poll! Hemlock can do what he likes. Why should *I* try to stop him?"

He turned away from the scene below and went to the stream to drink. With his face in the water, he found himself nose to nose with a plump trout. Much to his own surprise, he caught it with a sudden grab and flung it out onto the grass. Later he built a small fire and roasted the fish and ate it hungrily. Then he drank from the stream and stretched out in the sun to nap. He was extremely pleased with himself.

AYLEN WOKE FROM HIS NAP to an afternoon stillness so strange that for a moment he imagined the stream had stopped running, and sprang up to go and look. No, it spilled over its pebbles as eagerly as before— and here came another lazy fish. He made a trap with his fingers and caught it easily. But when he tossed it out onto the bank, its gasps were so loud in the new silence that he threw it back in horror. "Perhaps there's a storm coming," he said to himself. "It's often quiet just before a storm." But the sky was very blue, with only a few clouds, and those few hung motion- less. "Well, it feels like a storm, or *something*," he said aloud to Marrow, who was browsing about in the grass. "I think we'd better find some kind of shelter before nightfall." And he stared up uneasily at the hard blue sky.

There seemed no reason to go back down toward trouble. He headed Marrow up instead. They climbed for a long time and arrived at last at the very top of the mountain ridge. It was just as strangely silent here as below, and the few birches seemed less alive than the trees on the walls of Pitshaft's cave. Gaylen looked down on the kingdom, which lay streaked with shadows now as the sun dropped to the west.

From this height it looked calm and peaceful. "It isn't, though," he said to Marrow, "except maybe in the woldweller's oak or down in the mines with the dwarfs." He turned and peered over the other edge of the ridge, but the land on that side was lost in mist and offered nothing. Then he looked about him at the mountain top and shivered. There was a curious hollow in the stony ground at his feet, like a huge, shallow nest worn smooth from the whirl and settle of some gigantic, ancient bird. But there was no shelter anywhere beyond the motionless birches, nothing but the vast bowl of air above him and on either side the dropping away of rough slopes, which arched off ahead and behind into the blue smudge of distance. He felt as if he were perching on an enormous, narrow wall and had a sudden strong desire to hold on.

He went to sit against the trunk of a tree and tried to divert himself with his earlier anger, but the scowls and aches would not come. In their place was only a great wash of loneliness and isolation. "Where in the world do I belong?" he wondered. A solitary bird crossed high above and he looked up and watched it disappear. The silence was beginning to alarm him. He could hear the beat of his heart too plainly.

After a few moments he thought he heard something else, a faint, steady, rushing sound. He strained forward to listen. The rushing sound was very far away but clearly it was coming directly toward him through the air, with precise and frightening swiftness, as the ground comes toward you when you fall in a dream. It sped nearer and nearer and grew louder and louder. Gaylen could almost hear the smooth and terrible lift and fall of wings huge enough to rock the world. The leaves on the trees began to tremble. And still there was nothing to see but the purpling light of dusk. He pressed himself back against the tree trunk and waited with his eyes squeezed tight shut. The noise grew deliberately, relentlessly, and then, with a frightful shriek, it burst out of the sky and engulfed him. His hair was whipped about his head and the tree thrashed crazily. Then, just when he was sure he could bear it no longer, the shriek and rush dropped to a gentle murmur.

Gaylen opened his eyes warily, for his hair was still flying about a little and the leaves rustled. He could see nothing at all. Nevertheless, he was sure there was something there, just in front of him, hovering in the stony hollow. He could not have said what it was, for he seemed unable to do anything but look right through it.

"Who are you?" he cried, his heart pounding.

"Who are we?" a number of voices seemed to sing all together. "We are the wind, boy! We are the breeze and the blow, passing by, passing by. Sometimes we blow . . ." The voices rose to a shriek and the trees creaked while torn leaves whirled high into the air. "And sometimes we only breeze." They dropped to a low singsong. The leaves hung for an instant and then drifted gently down to settle on the ground at Gaylen's feet. "We flew away to race around the mountains," breathed the voices in the wind. "We swept the trees and rippled the lake.

She's weeping still, poor child; we dashed away her tears. And down below we puffed the foolish hats off foolish people's heads. They're fighting again, but not for long, for the streams are running dry. Soon there will be nothing but dust down below, just as it was in the oldest days."

"The streams are running dry?" echoed Gaylen stupidly. "But how?"

"He's doing it," sighed the voices, sifting the leaves at Gaylen's feet. "He's doing it at the lake, where all the waters begin. He wanted us to keep away the rains. Keep away the rains! We laughed at him. It's nothing to us, for the air is ours alone forever. Here in our nest we hatch our little zephyrs . . ." The voices crooned wordlessly for a moment and the grass swayed. "And then, if we like, we whirl up . . ." The voices rose again, and Gaylen covered his ears, turning his face away while his hair slapped against his cheeks and the birches groaned and dipped. "We whirl up," shrieked the voices, "and rush away!"

"Wait! Wait!" cried Gaylen suddenly. He struggled to stand up, his heart booming in his throat. "Take me with you! I want to go with you forever around the mountains!"

The voices screeched and spun with laughter. "You? You? You're only a man! Stay where you belong. You're nothing to us. We are wonderful, marvelous! We are the wind!" They rose higher still, to an ear-splitting scream, and with a great explosion of air which knocked Gaylen head over heels they were off across the tops of the mountains and gone.

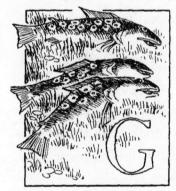

AYLEN SWAYED DIZZILY TO his feet as the voices of the wind shrieked away into the distance and faded. He stood for a long time gazing after them sadly. Then he remembered Marrow and looked about. The horse was nowhere to be seen. He ran up and down the narrow ridge, calling, but there was no answering whinny, no gentle thud of hoofs coming to meet him. The sun was rapidly disappearing behind the arc of mountains to his left and he felt a twinge of alarm. "Poor horse—he must have been frightened away when the wind came," he said to himself. "Maybe he went back to the stream." He started down the steep slope in the waning pink of sunset and after a long stumbling descent came at last, breathless and spent, to the spot where he and Marrow had rested in the afternoon. There, to be sure, was the horse, munching calmly in the shadows. Gaylen ran to him in relief and hugged him, and Marrow nuzzled gently into his shoulder. His warm, wet breath was as reassuring as an old friend's smile.

Gaylen stooped wearily to drink from the stream and immediately bumped his nose against the clammy back of another trout. Another trout? A dozen others. He drew back sharply and peered at the water in the half light. It was full of fish crowding downstream, their scales sparkling under the silver wash of a newly risen moon. And Gaylen saw that the stream itself was running shallower than it had that afternoon, was in fact dwindling. Then the wind was right. Hemlock—for it must be he—was somehow shutting off the water at its source and this little stream would soon be nothing but an empty, muddy trough. It must already be dry up above and the poor fish were following it down in a desperate search for deeper water. Gaylen plucked three from the scurrying host and laid them out on the grass for supper. "They'll probably all be dead soon anyway," he said to himself, trying to ignore a painful lump of pity that stretched his throat.

It occurred to him suddenly that the people of the kingdom were facing the same grim possibility. He stood and peered down in the moonlight. Far below, at the center of the valley floor, he could see the separate red eyes of a circle of campfires and he could just barely hear the sound of shouting and singing. Farther away to the left, a low hillside wore another bright circle of flames. "They've really begun the war," he said to himself. "And all over a word in a dictionary, the ninnies!"

He turned away and built a fire of his own and ate his supper of roasted fish with his back turned to the scene below. "Where in the world do I belong?" he wondered again. "Well, I don't belong down there," he said out loud. "Let Hemlock do what he wants." And then, "It's nothing to me."

 HEN GAYLEN HAD FINISHED his supper, he stomped out the campfire and stood thinking for a moment. Why

wait, he asked himself, and waste the moonlight, when he could be looking for Ardis and the lake? All he had to do was follow the stream up along the mountainside and he'd surely find both before long, for the wind had said that all the waters began there. Anyway, it was better to be moving than just sitting in the dark.

"Not that I'm lonesome, though, you know," he said to Marrow as they started off. "After all, I'm going to live alone now. That's been decided. It's just that I'm not tired enough to sleep." But after an hour or two of difficult riding along the slope, they were both too weary to go on. The moon had retired behind a bank of clouds, tucking its glow in under the edges. The night was left black, and there was so little water in the stream by now that they could no longer rely on its gurgle for a guide. "We'll stop at the first good spot we come to," Gaylen promised, and Marrow's ears twitched in reply. Before long they found a shallow, dry cave and soon both were sound asleep inside.

He woke quite suddenly in the middle of the night

and sat up, his eyes wide in the blackness. Surely that sound he had heard was too real to be part of a dream! The wind had returned and was flouncing about among the treetops, and the moon had emerged again to hang like a medallion against the dark sky. Gaylen poked his head out into the glow and listened. There it was again, something crashing along up the bank of the stream. In a few moments the silhouettes of two men on horseback appeared, riding slowly and talking in loud, daylight voices that sounded harsh and disrespectful against the hushed dignity of the night.

"We could have come over the mountains farther south. You've brought us miles out of our way!"

"Quit complaining, Murk. We can't work much till daylight anyway, and we'll be there by that time."

Silence. And then: "See here, Rankle. Are you sure this fellow Hemlock will do what he's promised? It's silly, stopping up that lake. No matter how strong we build the dam, it won't hold for long."

"He knows that. But he says he only needs a

couple of days for the people to run scared. They've been fighting a war anyway and they're already all in a pucker. He claims he's turned them against the King, so that when he gets control, by being the only one with water, they'll do what he says: kill the King and the court and crown him instead. He's going to make me General."

The other man gave a snort of derisive laughter. There was silence again and then he said, "Maybe it'll work, but he still sounds crack-brained to me."

"Of course he's crack-brained," said the first man. "He keeps talking about mermaids. But he's clever too, Murk. And it's a rich kingdom. We'd better hurry or the others will have the whole thing finished before we get there, and he'll change his mind about making me General." There was no more conversation. The two men spurred their horses and disappeared along the hillside into darkness.

Gaylen crouched in the cave listening to their hoofbeats die away. His tumbling thoughts clashed in a war of their own:

Hemlock wants to kill the King and the court!

And so? It's nothing to you.

But don't you see? That means the Prime Minister will be killed, too.

Yes, the old fool. He started it all, with his everlasting fried fish. Good riddance, I say.

He didn't really start it. At least, he didn't mean to. And anyway, he's my father.

He isn't your father.

Well, he's as good as a father any day. And I don't want him to be killed.

Why not? You're not going back to the castle anyway. You don't want to see any of them again. That's what you said. If you get involved in it now, you'll never get away afterwards. They won't let you.

I've got to try to save him. Don't you see? I can't just let him die. And there's Medley too. And Mrs. Copse. And . . .

Oh, for heaven's sake! I give you up. You wanted to help before and they threw things at you. You tried to explain and they wouldn't listen. And here you are, wanting to run right back into the middle of it.

I'll come away again afterwards. I'll say goodbye and come away again, back to the trees and the rocks and peace.

Never. You're too silly. You're a great baby. What became of all your fine anger and resolve?

I don't know! I have to go and try. I have to! I don't know why.

Gaylen sprang to his feet and dragged Marrow out of the cave. A moment later they were thrashing up along the hillside after the two men, up along the stream bed where the wet mud shone slickly in the bright moonlight. At last, just before dawn, he saw the light of torches up ahead and heard, against the trickle and splash of falling water, the crash of rocks being rolled about and the thud of an ax against complaining wood. Over it all, and floating into his senses as he came nearer, hung the wet, clean smell of reeds and moss, the muddy fragrance of lily pads, the damp freshness of breezes that have spent the night skimming over cool, dark water. He had come at last, with the whistle round his neck, to the lake.

AYLEN CLIMBED CAREFUL-ly down from Marrow's back and tied the horse to a sapling beside the muddy stream bed. Then he crept forward from rock to tree trunk, as near as he dared—and stared. In the first faint light of dawn, he saw the whole scene clearly. Before him, in a huge cup of cliffs, lay the lake, glimmering away into shadow, surrounded by a broad rim of trees and grass that tilted up, far to his right, to the top of the mountain ridge. To his left, where the mountainside sloped down to the valley floor, the rim of grass around the lake was very narrow and here there was a V-shaped gap, like a chip cracked out of the edge of the cup.

Below the V the beds of many streams fanned out and disappeared among the rocks. Some, like the one he had followed, angled off to the sides, while others curved down the slope to the kingdom below. This, then, was where the lake water had been spilling over for hundreds of years, spilling over and rushing down with life for trees and grass and animals and people in every drop.

But now, by the light of torches, a great many men, their shadows huge and menacing, were laboring to dam up the water. They had wedged a great cross of stout tree trunks into the V and were cramming rocks and branches and mud into the chinks. Now and then water would burst through somewhere in a shining jet and with yells and curses the men would attack the weak spot and reinforce it with more mud and branches. Above them, on the rim at the top of the dam, a figure paced, shouting instructions. Hemlock.

Gaylen watched from behind a row of boulders not twenty yards away, listening to Hemlock's shouts and the water splashing through the last few chinks. From below, one of the men called, "I don't like the looks of that bottom rock!"

"It'll hold," cried Hemlock. "Give it more mud and it'll hold. Long enough, anyway."

Long enough! The words were chilling. Long enough to stop the water, to parch the people's throats, to turn them in their thirst toward the murder of the King. Long enough to alter everything. "You've got nothing that lasts, you know." The woldweller's words came back to him. "But this tree has stood here all along. What do you make of that, boy?"

Through this memory he saw again the fond and gentle face of the Prime Minister and his heart gave a wrench. He looked up at the trees over his head and sighed. "It's easy for you to stand there all along. You don't know how it feels to care about anything. Why, you don't even care about not caring!"

Suddenly, just as the sun lifted over the eastern

arc of the mountains, there was a silence so absolute that Gaylen was jarred back to the scene before him. He held his breath. The splashing had stopped. Hemlock stood frozen for a moment, listening, and then he threw up his arms and yelled a great yell of triumph that rang and echoed against the cliffs.

"I've done it!" he shouted. "It works! The water is stopped and the kingdom is mine!"

AYLEN SANK DOWN BEHIND the boulder. He was very, very tired. He rubbed his forehead with his fingertips and wondered what to do. The dam was complete, the water was stopped, and Hemlock and his men would be watching it and guarding it. How in the world could he save anybody? If only the cockatoo would come. He counted out the days on his fingers. Yes, it was Wednesday again. Perhaps the cockatoo would find him and then he could send back a warning. Perhaps the King and the court could escape over the mountains to the north. Perhaps, if there was time.

The sun was rising fast and the morning sky was hard and cloudless. It was going to be hot, one of those breathless, burning days that sometimes come along early to scout the way for summer. How convenient for Hemlock, thought Gaylen. People would grow thirsty quickly on a day like this. They would turn from their war and hurry to find water at the lake. And then . . .

He shook off the thought and remembered Marrow, tied among the trees below with nothing to drink. At least he could save one creature from thirst. He crept away, down to where the horse stood motionless beside the stream bed, and led him up, circling wide around the V where Hemlock and his men were resting now, and came to the banks of the lake well behind, out of their sight and hearing. Here, under the willows, he sat barefoot at the water's edge and cooled his toes while Marrow drank. There was nothing to do but wait. Wait for the cockatoo, and wait for the people of the kingdom to come scrambling up the mountainside to find—Hemlock and the dam.

Gaylen stretched out on his stomach and gazed at the lake. It lay before him blue and flat and smooth as a mirror, half a mile across to where the clear reflections of trees and cliffs on the other side hung upside down and motionless. Here and there the upturned palms of lily pads were starred with white blossoms, and he was reminded suddenly of the water lily in Pitshaft's cave, reminded of the carved curling fingers that held it, reminded at last of Ardis. He drew the whistle-key out from his jerkin and turned it over in his fingers, wondering about the mermaid. Where was she now? Would she come if he blew the whistle? Maybe she would help him if he gave the whistle back. He sat up, grasping the whistle in his fist. If he were to blow the whistle, Ardis might come and . . .

Just at that moment he heard a faraway squawk. The cockatoo! He sprang up and ran out from under the trees, searching the sky for the white speck. And there it was, circling high over the lake. He longed to call out to it, but he was afraid Hemlock would hear him, so he stood on a rock and waved his arms frantically. At last the cockatoo seemed to see him, and it started down in a wide spiral. Then Gaylen heard shouting from lower down. Hemlock had seen it too, had seen it and must know what bird it was. The shouts came nearer and suddenly there was a twang and a hum and a soft thud and the cockatoo fell like a stone at Gaylen's feet, an arrow through its breast.

Gaylen barely had time to snatch the paper from its leg and race back to the trees before Hemlock and one of his men, bow in hand, burst out from the rocks and ran to where the dead bird lay. "That's what it was, all right," said Hemlock. "Bringing that boy a message, I suppose. He'll be somewhere nearby, then. Come, let's see if we can find him."

Gaylen sprang into the branches of the first likely willow and climbed swiftly up and up until he was hidden among the leaves. Only then did he stop, gasping for breath, torn between sorrow for the cockatoo and anger at Hemlock's cruelty. He could hear the men searching far below. After a few moments Hemlock cried triumphantly, "Here's his horse! We'll take it back with us. He can't get far without it, and even if he could, there's nothing he can do now. We can't spend the day looking for him—we've got to keep watch over the dam." Gaylen heard their footsteps and the soft thump of Marrow's hoofs fade away through the trees.

He balanced himself against a forked branch and stared fixedly up at the leaves over his head, gritting his teeth to fight back hot tears. Hemlock was right. There was nothing he could do now. Unless Ardis— but it was foolish to pin his hopes on a mermaid. "Ardis is only a dream," Hemlock had said many days ago, and perhaps it was true. All of them, the woldweller, the dwarfs, the voices in the wind, all were probably dreams, now that he came to think about it. He rubbed his eyes fiercely and opened the Prime Minister's letter:

Vaungaylen: The King rides out today to reason with the people. All the streams are going dry, as you must know wherever you are. We hear from our scouts that Hemlock is damming up the lake. The King is sure this will prove to the people that Hemlock is behind it all and hopes to lead them to some resolution of the trouble. The war has not amounted to much as yet, I'm glad to say, for they have no leaders and are very disorganized. But we must get to them soon, for they are angry and confused. I'm coming, too. Perhaps we'll meet at the lake. I pray for your safety, my dear. *The P.M.*

GAYLEN CLIMBED WEARILY down out of the tree and wandered over to the edge of the lake. There he stretched out full length and dipped his hot face into the cool water. What good would it do, he wondered, if the King should ride up to the dam? Hemlock's men could kill him themselves with their bows and arrows and spare Hemlock the trouble of churning up the people to do it. The cockatoo would carry no more messages, no matter how important, poor thing. Even Marrow was lost to him now. He sighed and closed his eyes. And then, because he was young and had not closed his eyes in many hours, he slept while the hot sun rolled silently up across the sky and even the birds seemed to wait in their nests.

When he woke, the sun had crossed, dropped, and disappeared, and it was night. Overhead, the moon hung round as the eye of an owl and the sky was bright with stars. A light breeze stirred the drooping branches of the willows. He could see, far around the brim of the lake, the red halo of a fire where Hemlock and his men kept watch over the dam. So the people hadn't come. Not yet. Then they would doubtless come tomorrow. He stood up and stretched and wandered back along the bank to where a flat rock jutted out dimly over the water, and here among the shadowed reeds he sat watching the moon's reflection glow and splinter and glow again as the breeze furrowed the surface of the lake. Through his mind ran the words of the minstrel's song:

> *Two moons wander where the water curls,*
> *Two white moons in a pair of skies—*
> *Two moons yonder like a pair of pearls*
> *There by the lake where the water swirls.*

Yes, he thought to himself, that was just the way it looked. Only, one of the skies was upside down. "It's really the sky *I'm* under that's upside down," he said aloud, "and I'm upside down too, and so is the whole world. It must be, for everything to be so wrong."

After a moment or two, as he sat there, he had the curious feeling that someone was watching him. He turned his head cautiously and saw two wide, shining eyes staring up at him from the reeds that fringed the rock. Just as he looked into them, there was a soft splash and the eyes disappeared.

"Ardis!" he whispered. "Ardis, come back!" His heart thumped in his throat and he called again, very softly, "Ardis! I've brought you back your whistle!" He waited, holding his breath. Soon there was another little splash and the eyes appeared again, this time on the other side of the rock.

"Ardis!" His breath caught. Not a dream! Not a dream after all. With trembling hands he fumbled at his jerkin and, pulling the whistle and chain over his head, he held them up in the moonlight. "Oh, Ardis, see? I've brought the whistle back to you!"

Two small hands reached up and parted the reeds, and there before him was the round and lovely face of the mermaid in Pitshaft's cave, only ever so much more lovely than the cold stone could ever have conveyed. And she was very young, like Medley; only a child, with her long hair curling wet and heavy over her narrow shoulders. How could she be so young, wondered Gaylen as he gazed at her, when she was so very, very old? Had she really been weeping for hundreds of years? How sad she looked! But he said to himself, "I must try to get her to help me save the King, for she'll be just as indifferent as the others if I let her be."

"Ardis!" he said aloud. "Come and tell me about the whistle, for there's much I don't understand. And then, if you'll do a favor for me, I'll give it back to you."

The mermaid stared at the whistle and then looked searchingly at Gaylen. At last, after a long moment, she placed her little hands on the edge of the rock and, with a lithe twist, flipped herself up beside him. She was small and light and smelled of lilies, and her long tail, glittering with its myriad bright scales, curled gracefully under her. Gaylen was quite dizzy with admiration as he looked at her, but he kept his voice firm. "Tell me, Ardis," he said. "Tell me about the whistle."

"I am the guardian of the spring that feeds the lake," said the mermaid, in a voice so low and soft that he had to bend close to distinguish it from the lap of the water around the rock. "The dwarfs made a house over the spring. The door to the house opens and closes by the sound of the whistle. Bevel made the whistle, and he made my pretty doll too, long ago. But one day a man came and took my whistle and blew it." She paused to take a breath and two big tears rolled down her cheeks. "The door to the spring house closed and my doll was locked inside. And then he took my whistle away. I've wept for my whistle and my doll for a long time. I want my doll. Give me back my whistle!" And she put out her little hand to take it.

But Gaylen held the whistle out of reach, feeling heartless but determined. "So that's how it was," he said. "Yes, I'll give you the whistle, but first you must promise to do a task for me."

"What do you want me to do?" asked the mermaid, her eyes never leaving the whistle where it swung from Gaylen's hand.

"You must swim to the front of the lake," said Gaylen slowly and clearly. "You must swim down to the dam the men have built and loosen the stones so the water will flow out again."

"But why must I do that?" said Ardis. "What has that to do with me?"

"Nothing." He said it for her: "It's nothing to you. But it's much to me. I won't give you the whistle until you promise."

"I promise," said the mermaid, watching the whistle. Gaylen looked at her and felt a surge of doubt. Her face was pale and lovely in the dim light, but her wide eyes were as deep and unreadable as the waters of the lake. "I should have made her do it now, before I give her the whistle," he said to himself, "but it's too late—too cruel to keep it from her now."

"You must really do it if you promise to," he said to her.

"I promise," she repeated. He sighed and with a shrug dropped the whistle and its chain into her waiting hand. She trembled slightly and put the whistle to her lips. Gaylen heard no sound, but from somewhere nearby came a startled croak and a great black crow rose swiftly from the shadows farther down the bank and flapped across the water. With a little cry of joy, Ardis dropped the chain over her head, flipped off the rock and disappeared into the lake.

Gaylen strained forward to watch. After a few moments, far out from the bank, the water bubbled and a white arm was thrust up. He caught a glimpse of a little doll, its linked stone body clinking as the hand that clutched it gave it a shake. Then the arm sank below the surface, taking the doll with it, and there was nothing left but a widening circle of ripples.

AYLEN SAT IN THE MOON-
light beside the lake and
thought about all that had happened since the day

the poll began. Past his mind's eye streamed all the faces he had seen, all the kind, angry, laughing, anxious faces that had peopled the days of his great adventure. And he remembered, too, those others: the woldweller's gray cheeks fixed into furrows like the bark of a tree; the dwarfs, impassive and calm as the mountains themselves; the wind that spoke through a hundred wayward, invisible mouths; and Ardis with her eyes wet and unfathomable as the lake that glimmered before him. He leaned over and studied the dim reflection of his own face in the water. Young and skinny, he decided, and tired and worried, too. A transient, changeable, ageable face. A people face. "And that's where I belong," he said to himself at last.

He stood up and made his way back around the edge of the lake to the dam, and here he sat down behind a boulder to wait for morning. The dam was holding firm. Ardis had not kept her promise. He could see Hemlock's campfire just beyond the dam on the other side of the V, and two hunched figures, silhouetted against the glow, keeping watch.

"It's going well so far," said the man called Rankle. "Tomorrow I'll be a General!"

"I've waited a long time for this," came Hemlock's voice in reply, "and planned it all with great care. It's all worked out just as I wanted it to, except for one thing."

"What's that?" asked Rankle.

"Ardis. I never found her. I never got to talk to her. She could ruin it all if she took a mind to."

"Ardis?" said Rankle. "Who's Ardis?"

"Never mind," said Hemlock. "You'd never understand."

They were quiet then. Gaylen dozed behind his boulder and tried not to think about what the morning would bring. But when the long night had passed and the sky began to brighten once again, he opened his eyes and felt his throat tighten. There could not be much longer to wait. As the sun flooded the mountainside with sudden gold, a bird chirped happily. But Gaylen didn't hear it. He sat tensely and listened for a different sound. And after what seemed like hours, he heard it—the rumble of a hundred horses' hoofs and the clear call of a horn. The people were coming at last.

U P FROM THE VALLEY FLOOR, along the muddy stream beds and over the rocks they came, on horses and mules and on foot, all the men of the kingdom and the fiercer women too, in every sort of costume, with every sort of weapon. They were dusty and thirsty and tired. And they were angry. At the head rode the King, proud and severe, the sunlight flashing from his crown, and his horse splendid in red brocade. On his left rode the General, scowling in heavy chain mail, and on his right, uneasy in his saddle but with chin raised firmly over tousled beard, rode the Prime Minister. Just behind them came the army, twenty sober men in leather helmets, with spears held erect. The royal banner fluttered red and black in the breeze and the horn sounded again and again.

Gaylen forgot his anxiety. He sprang out from behind the boulder and waved his arms. *"Eee-ow!"* he yelled, and went bounding recklessly down the mountainside to meet them. Tripping and stumbling, he ran, and all at once an arrow flashed down and ripped through his sleeve, narrowly missing his arm.

The crowd surging up toward the dam stopped in alarm and the horn was silenced. "Gaylen!" wailed the Prime Minister, sliding down from his horse's back.

"I'm all right!" cried Gaylen, and he ran the last few yards and flung his arms around the Prime Minister's neck.

"You're here at last," shouted a deep voice. All eyes turned up and there stood Hemlock, triumphant, on the top of the dam.

There was a moment's silence. Then angry yells

burst from the crowd and the soldiers lifted their spears. But Hemlock raised an arm. "If you make a move toward me," he shouted, "the King will be shot. My men are posted here and their bows are drawn."

"It's true! Watch out!" cried Gaylen. "They're up there behind the rocks."

"Now, by Harry!" bellowed the King, nudging his horse a step nearer. "What do you think you're doing up there?"

"I'm waiting," said Hemlock. He bent and scooped up a handful of water from the lake behind him and splashed his wet palm across his lips. "Hot, isn't it?" he cried. "Are you thirsty?" The people sighed and licked their lips and the animals strained against their ropes and reins. The sun, as if in league with Hemlock, burned from the sky and the rocks wavered and shone with heat. Hemlock scooped another handful of water and drank noisily. He let the drops trickle down his chin, grinning at the crowd. Then his eyes narrowed. "I will be King," he shouted, "one way or another. People! Seize the King and the others and kill them and I'll open the dam. Seize him! If you don't, my men will have to kill him and many of you as well. And I can hold the dam for days while you wait and die!"

The people muttered and the General cried, "Never, Hemlock! Never in the world!"

But Hemlock ignored him. "People!" he shouted. "Your crops are withering. Your animals are gasping. And your children—don't you care for your children? Your children are weeping for water. People! Your children are *dying!*"

The crowd moaned and surged forward toward the King, and his face, under the shining crown, went white. Gaylen pressed his fists against his cheeks. "Ardis!" he whispered. "Oh, Ardis, do it now."

There was a sudden grinding noise. At the bottom of the dam a plug of mud loosened and a little jet of water spurted out. The crowd paused. Then the grinding noise came again and a great stone below the cross of tree trunks holding up the dam began to turn slowly.

"Look out!" yelled someone. "The dam is breaking!"

Suddenly the great stone burst loose. With a thunderous roar it leapt out in a huge arc of mud and drenching foam. A tumble of logs and branches was wrenched free and the dam collapsed. There was a terrible scream and Hemlock was thrown down, down among the rocks, and the water of the lake boiled over and around him and surged again, with a hiss of bubbles, into its old, accustomed channels.

AT THE FIRST SIGN OF DANger, the people had scrambled to get out of the way, and now they stood about on rocks and fallen logs, shaken and silent, watching the water surge down the mountainside, flooding the banks of its old stream beds and carving new ones as it went. But before long the lake was restored to its usual level and the streams were calmed. From the rocks at one side of the V, where the water had tossed him, Hemlock groaned. And they heard at the same time the sound of hoofbeats somewhere up above, as the men who had helped him fled away. But the King sat apart on his horse, his head bowed.

A man sprang forward into the middle of the nearest stream and Gaylen recognized him. It was Veto, the mayor of the second town. "Long live the King!" yelled Veto, and instantly the cry was taken up and the mountains rang: "Long live the King!"

The King raised his head and looked about him. Then he smiled and held up his hand. "Drink!" he shouted. "It's all over, by Harry! Go and drink."

And all of a sudden everybody was in the water, splashing and laughing and slipping on the rocks, drenched instantly from head to foot. Gaylen stood with the Prime Minister and the General near the King's horse and watched, grinning with relief. "Delicious!" a man called to his neighbors, and they answered, "Yes, yes, delicious," and bent to drink again.

"Why, listen to that!" said the King. "There's your definition, DeCree. After today no one could ever disagree with it."

"You're right!" exclaimed the Prime Minister. "I do believe you're right. That's it, of course. That's it at last! 'Delicious is a drink of cool water when you're very, very thirsty.' " And they all laughed and clapped each other on the back.

The people were beginning to disperse now, hurrying away down the mountainside to return to their children, their farms, their own concerns. The King sat for a moment, watching them go, and then he sent his soldiers to bring Hemlock down from the rocks and carry him back to the castle. "A pity he wasn't killed," said the King to the Prime Minister. "Now I suppose we'll have to nurse his broken bones and clutter up the dungeon with him."

"Banish him when he's well again. That's my advice," said the Prime Minister. Then suddenly he asked, "Vaungaylen, where's my cockatoo?"

"He's dead," answered Gaylen. "Hemlock's men shot him. I'm sorry."

"Dead," echoed DeCree. "Oh, dear." He stared down sadly at the ground. "All this trouble—the poll, the war, and this business today—and nobody killed. All safe and sound. Except for my poor, blameless bird."

"We'll put up a statue to it," the King declared. "A lovely little statue in the garden. To help us remember."

They stood together quietly for a long moment, each with his own thoughts, and then Gaylen climbed back up to the lake and found Marrow where Hemlock had tied him under the trees. He pressed his cheek against the horse's neck and stood gazing out across the sparkling water. "She must be happy now," he said to Marrow. "I'm glad she has her whistle back again." He sighed. "I wonder if she kept her promise after all or if it just happened all by itself. I guess," he said, "I'll never know. Come on, old friend, we're going home."

W ELL," SAID THE PRIME MIN-ister as they all sat down to supper at the castle. "It certainly is a relief to have all that nonsense over with. Now I can finish up my dictionary in peace."

"So you can, at that," said the King. "What comes next, after Delicious?"

"Oh, I'm way past the D's," said the Prime Minister. "As a matter of fact, I've got to the G's. I've just done Golden. 'Golden is the setting sun.' How's that?"

"You can't be serious," said the King. "Setting suns are pink. Everyone knows that. Why not say 'Golden is a ripe lemon'?"

The Queen took a sip of wine and said, "Excuse me, my dear, but lemons are yellow. 'Lemon yellow' is how the phrase goes. As for Golden, I'd rather see it read 'Golden is a clump of daffodils.' "

"Or 'Golden is a mug of beer,' " suggested the General.

"Now, by Harry," said the King, "I won't have it. Let DeCree say what he wants, can't you? 'Golden is a ripe lemon' will do perfectly well."

" 'Golden is the setting sun' is what I was planning to say," put in the Prime Minister. He sighed heavily. "Writing a dictionary is certainly no bed of roses."

"No bed of *daffodils*," murmured the Queen.

Gaylen got up from his place and wandered unnoticed to the window while the argument at the table went on. He leaned out and gazed at the countryside where it rolled away blue and purple in the twilight. The mountains sprawled comfortably across the horizon and from behind a smudge of quiet clouds the waning moon peeped out and touched the dark treetops with silver. Somewhere out there, he thought to himself, the woldweller was peacefully roasting a rabbit. Pitshaft would be playing the flute now by torchlight, while Bevel danced his calm, unhurried dance through the curling smoke from Thwart's tobacco. Ardis would be splashing softly about in the dark, still waters of the lake, her doll in her arms. And the wind—well, the wind was off somewhere around the mountains, but a newly hatched zephyr breathed in at the window and ruffled Gaylen's hair. In the room behind him, the argument continued. The King thumped on the table with his fist while the Queen's voice rose shrill and insistent over the General's growls, and Gaylen yearned again toward the unencumbered land beyond. Then he heard the Prime Minister calling to him.

"Gaylen! Vaungaylen, dear boy, come and sit by me and eat your supper."

His heart warmed then, and he smiled. "I'll go out again from time to time," he whispered, "but just at the moment..."

"Gaylen, my boy!" called the Prime Minister again.

"I'm coming," answered Gaylen happily. "I was just getting a breath of fresh air."

"The air *is* fresh tonight, by Harry," said the King. "Fresh as a daisy."

"Fresh as a *daffodil!*" murmured the Queen.

EPILOGUE

ONE DAY IN EARLY SPRING a bearded minstrel stopped at the castle and asked for "the young poll-taker." At first no one knew whom he meant. A page was sent to fetch the Prime Minister, who came creakily to the gate.

"We've only had one poll in this kingdom," said the Prime Minister, "and that was thirteen years ago. So it must be Vaungaylen you're after."

"Yes," said the minstrel, "that was the boy's name."

"Well, he's a boy no longer," said the Prime Minister. "He's a man now, twenty-five years old. He's got a child of his own. A little daughter." And he beamed with pride.

"Where can I find him?" asked the minstrel.

"He lives in the first town," said DeCree. "He's the Mayor there. He married the Mayor's daughter, Medley, and now he's the Mayor himself." And he beamed again.

"Thank you," said the minstrel. "I'll go along and find him."

"Oh, you won't find him there now," said DeCree.

"No? Why not?"

"It's April," answered DeCree.

"April?" The minstrel was clearly puzzled.

"Yes. You see," said the Prime Minister, "he goes away every April."

"Where does he go?" the minstrel wanted to know.

"Well, he goes into the forest, he and Medley and the child. And he goes up in the mountains and around the lake." The Prime Minister peered off through the gate and sniffed the warm spring air.

"Why does he do that?" asked the minstrel.

"It all started with the poll, thirteen years ago," said the Prime Minister. He frowned. "It's a strange story. There are parts of it that I've never . . . Well, it's a very strange story." He stopped and squinted at the minstrel. "Now that I come to think of it, you might be interested, a man in your profession." He took the minstrel by the arm and drew him into the courtyard. "Come in, come in. I'll tell you all about it. It just might be you'd want to make a song about it. It would make a pretty song," he added as they disappeared into the castle, "a very pretty song."

GOFISH

What did you want to be when you grew up?
When I was a preschooler, I wanted to be a pirate, and then when I started school, I wanted to be a librarian. But in the fourth grade, I got my copy of *Alice in Wonderland / Alice Through the Looking-Glass* and decided once and for all that I wanted to be an illustrator of stories for children.

When did you realize you wanted to be a writer?
I didn't even think about writing. My husband wrote the story for the first book. But then he didn't want to do it anymore, so I had to start writing my own stories. After

all, you can't make pictures for stories unless you have stories to make pictures for.

What's your first childhood memory?
I have a lot of preschool memories, all from when we lived in a little town just south of Columbus, Ohio. I kind of remember sitting in a high chair. And when I was a little older, I remember seeing Jack Frost looking in through the kitchen window. *That* was pretty surprising.

What's your most embarrassing childhood memory?
I don't remember any. I'm probably just suppressing them all.

What's your favorite childhood memory?
I think I liked best the times when my sister and I would curl up next to our mother while she read aloud to us.

As a young person, who did you look up to most?
No question: my mother.

What was your worst subject in school?
Arithmetic. I think you call it math now.

What was your best subject in school?
Art. And after that, English.

What was your first job?

It was when I was a teenager. I worked in what we called the College Shop in a big downtown Cleveland (Ohio) department store called Higbee's. But after that, I mostly worked in the pricing department of a washing machine factory.

How did you celebrate publishing your first book?

I don't think I did anything special. By that time, I was beginning to get over my absolute astonishment at having found my editor in the *first* place. That was the most wonderful moment of all.

Where do you write your books?

I think about them for a long time before I actually start putting words on paper, and I think about them all over the place. Then, when I'm ready, I work at my computer in my workroom. But before, I always wrote them out longhand, sitting on my sofa in the living room. I wrote on a big tablet, and then I typed everything, paragraph by paragraph, on my typewriter, making changes as I went along.

Where do you find inspiration for your writing?

I mostly write about all the unanswered questions I still have from when I was in elementary school.

Which of your characters is most like you?
The main characters in all of my long stories are like me,
but I think Winnie Foster, in *Tuck Everlasting,* is most like
me.

When you finish a book, who reads it first?
Always my editor, Michael di Capua. His opinion is the
most important one.

Are you a morning person or a night owl?
Neither one, really. I'm mostly a middle-of-the-day person.

What's your idea of the best meal ever?
One that someone else cooked. And it has to have
something chocolate for dessert.

Which do you like better: cats or dogs?
Cats to look at and to watch, but dogs to own.

What do you value most in your friends?
Good talk and plenty of laughing.

Where do you go for peace and quiet?
Now that my children are grown and gone into lives of
their own, I have plenty of peace and quiet just sitting
around the house.

What makes you laugh out loud?
Words. My father was very funny with words, and I grew up laughing at the things he said.

What's your favorite song?
Too many to mention, but most of them are from the '30s and '40s, when songs were to *sing*, not to shout and wiggle to.

Who is your favorite fictional character?
No question: Alice from *Alice in Wonderland* and *Alice Through the Looking-Glass*.

What are you most afraid of?
I have a fear that is very common when we are little, and I seem to have hung on to it: the fear of being abandoned.

What time of year do you like best?
May is my favorite month.

What is your favorite TV show?
I don't watch many shows anymore—just CNN News and old movies.

If you were stranded on a desert island, who would you want for company?
My husband, Sam.

If you could travel in time, where would you go?
Back to Middletown, Ohio, to Lincoln School on Central Avenue, to live through fifth grade again. And again and again.

What's the best advice you have ever received about writing?
No one single thing. Too many good things to list.

What do you want readers to remember about your books?
The questions without answers.

What would you do if you ever stopped writing?
Spend all my time doing word puzzles and games, and practicing the good old songs on my piano.

What do you like best about yourself?
That I can draw, and play the good old songs on my piano.

What is your worst habit?
Always expecting things to be perfect.

What is your best habit?
Trying to make things as perfect as I can.

SQUARE FISH

What do you consider to be your greatest accomplishment?

Right now, it's a picture for a new book that hasn't even been published yet. It's a picture of a man in a washtub, floating on the ocean in a rainstorm. I'm really proud of that picture.

Where in the world do you feel most at home?

That's a hard question. My family moved away from Middletown, Ohio (see the question/answer about time travel), when I was in the middle of sixth grade, and we never went back. Even after all these years, though, Middletown is the place I think of when I think about "home." I've lived in a lot of different places, though, and liked them all, so I don't feel sorry for myself. It's just that the word "home" has its own kind of special meaning.

What do you wish you could do better?

Everything. Cook, write, play the piano, everything.

What would your readers be most surprised to learn about you?

Maybe that I believe that writing books is a long way from being important. The most important thing anyone can do is be a teacher. As for those of us who write books, I often think we should all stop for fifty years. There are so many wonderful books to read, and not enough time to get around to all of them. But we writers just keep cranking them out. All we can hope for is that readers will find at least a little time for them, anyway.

SQUARE FISH